℧

R

M

"Oh—what a fool I was," she fumed.

Harriet took a deep breath to steady herself. "How many days and nights do you intend to keep me prisoner?"

Richard just sat silently, his eyes studying her through the curling smoke of his cigar.

"At least tell me why you have brought me here."

The indifference on his face was galling. "To punish you for what someone else suffered at your hands."

His words astounded her. "I have no idea what you're talking about!"

It was all so unreal. The man had virtually kidnapped her! The worst was, he'd deluded her into thinking he was falling in love with her—allowing her to fall for him—that was the real turn of the knife.

CATHERINE GEORGE was born in Wales, and following her marriage to an engineer, lived eight years in Brazil at a gold mine site, an experience she would later draw upon for her books. It was not until she and her husband returned to England and bought a village post office and general store that she submitted her first book at her husband's encouragement. Now her husband helps manage their household so that Catherine can devote more time to her writing. They have two children, a daughter and a son, who share their mother's love of language and writing.

Books by Catherine George

HARLEQUIN PRESENTS

HARLEQUIN ROMANCE

CATHERINE GEORGE

GEORGE

the marriage bed

Harlequin Books

TORONTO • NEW YORK • LONDON
AMSTERDAM • PARIS • SYDNEY • HAMBURG
STOCKHOLM • ATHENS • TOKYO • MILAN

Harlequin Presents first edition July 1987
ISBN 0-373-10992-X

Original hardcover edition published in 1986
by Mills & Boon Limited

CHAPTER ONE

THE miracle happened on a chilly afternoon in spring.
Harriet was washing her hands in the cloakroom of the
Acme Mail Order Company, and shivering because the
temperature inside the building was colder than that of
the brisk day outside, her employer not the man to waste
money on heating now that April was here. It was his
voice that interrupted her, as usual, over the intercom
relayed through all parts of the building, and Harriet
looked up at the small loudspeaker with dislike before
deliberately turning back to the mirror to retie the stock
at the collar of her crisp white shirt before walking
without haste along the corridor leading past the glassed-
in typists' pool to the door marked 'Managing Director'.

As she knocked and went in Harvey Jackson looked
up from his desk, which, like everything in the large
room, was the latest thing in executive furnishing. He
waved Harriet to a contorted arrangement of tubes and
leather and she sat down, rather taken aback. The chair
was hideous, uncomfortable and gave the occupant an
unavoidable confrontation with the garish cubist painting on the wall opposite, but it was nevertheless the one
normally reserved for visitors.

'Ah—thought you were lost, Miss Neil,' he said with
chilling jocularity. 'You were missing from your office.'

'I was in the cloakroom, Mr Jackson.'

'Yes, of course.' He never apologised for interrupting
her there, even though in her eighteen months as his
personal assistant Harriet had rarely achieved an
undisturbed trip to the cloakroom unless Harvey Jackson
was absent from the building. She waited expectantly,
but he went on fiddling with a letter-opener, and was
obviously avoiding the question in her dark eyes.

5

'I believe I'm right in saying you've not taken a holiday during the past year,' he said eventually, which was just about the last thing she had expected him to say.

'No, I haven't, Mr Jackson.' And well you know it, she added silently, stiffening as he looked her straight in the eye. This, as she knew of old, was a bad sign. He must be trying to break something unpleasant to her.

'My mother-in-law has suddenly been taken ill,' he stated.

Harriet's eyelids flickered. 'I'm sorry to hear that,' she said, surprised. Harvey Jackson was not in the habit of discussing personal matters with her.

'She was—er—on the point of going on holiday—my little treat to her,' he continued.

'How unfortunate.'

'Yes. Seems to have caught this virus that's been going the rounds.'

I caught it too, thought Harriet bitterly, only you never even noticed because I staggered to work with mine.

'The thing is, Miss Neil, I thought it might be a good idea if you went in her place,' went on her employer, and subjected his pristine blotter to an intense scrutiny.

Harriet kept her mouth from falling open only by effort. 'Me, Mr Jackson? But——'

'Free of charge,' he interrupted, and looked her in the eye again. 'Hotel Miramar in Praia do Ceu. The Algarve, you know. Very nice this time of the year.'

Harriet could well believe it. It was the free of charge bit she found hard to swallow.

'But surely you could get a refund, Mr Jackson?'

He shook his head regretfully. 'Too late. The flight's on Sunday.'

'Sunday! But today's Thursday, Mr Jackson. I couldn't possibly——'

'Why not, Miss Neil?' His jaw set obstinately. 'It's a convenient time here since the autumn catalogue is well in hand, and Miss What's-her-name from the typing pool—the one with the red hair—can fill in for you while you're away, and I understand you have no—er— commitments on the social side at the moment.'

This time Harriet was dumbfounded. How on earth did he know that? Her most recent emotional relationship had just come to an abrupt end, it was true, but she could have sworn no one in the company knew.

'I thought you might be glad of a break,' concluded Harvey Jackson, and favoured her with the rather unsettling show of teeth he employed as a smile.

Ten minutes later Harriet was back in her own office, feeling dazed and incredulous. Like an automaton she signed the mountain of routine letters from the typing pool, her mind working furiously. A free holiday in Portugal was not to be sneezed at—only a fool would pass it up. And though she might be considered many things by the other employees of the Alpha Mail Order Company, she knew very well fool was not one of them. The members of the typing pool, to a woman, had been with the firm for years and were all jealous and resentful of Harriet, every girl there believing the job of personal assistant to Mr Jackson should have gone to one of them, not a newcomer like the much too decorative Miss Neil. The only people in the firm with whom Harriet had any rapport at all were in the accounts department and all male, which did nothing to endear her to her critics.

The more she thought about Harvey Jackson's offer the more unbelievable it seemed, and after ten minutes of scribbling her signature on credit slips and various answers to complaints she marched back into his office.

'Mr Jackson,' she began, 'I've thought it over and I really don't feel I can accept a free holiday, tempting though the offer is.'

He rose to his feet, his eyes cold. 'I assure you there is nothing shady about it, Miss Neil.'

'No, no, of course not,' she said hurriedly. 'It's just that it seems such a lot of money——'

His unnerving smile stopped her mid-sentence. 'Look

upon it as a bonus in recognition of all the extra work you put in for me.'

And never get paid for, thought Harriet. Put like that it seemed reasonable, if totally uncharacteristic. 'Then thank you, Mr Jackson. I accept with gratitude.' She smiled at him and took the envelope he handed over.

'It's all there, Miss Neil. Air flight from Birmingham, two weeks at the Miramar in one of their best rooms. English spoken by most of the staff, I believe.'

'It's such a marvellous surprise.' Harriet looked at the bulging envelope and shook her head in wonder. 'It's so very kind of you. Now perhaps I'd better see Hazel Bishop in the typing pool and give her a teach-in on my routine.'

'Don't mention I'm involved,' said Harvey Jackson sharply. 'You know how it is—small firm like this; gossip, I mean. Can't be too careful, can one?'

Harriet's eyes narrowed. 'Of course, Mr Jackson. I won't breathe a word.'

What was he up to? she wondered uneasily as she finished off the mail. Luxury holidays could hardly fall off the back of a lorry, and this one was with a highly reputable tour firm—none of your bucket-shop specials. Perhaps Mr J. had won it, or been given it in return for a little favour of his own to someone. She wouldn't put it past him. Harriet's job was interesting and she enjoyed it, but like her employer she could not. He was quite attractive, in a sharp-featured rather flashy way, fair and slim and forty-ish, but there was some indefinable something about him she just couldn't stick at any price. Whatever it was affected only herself, seemingly, as all the other females in the firm thought he was God's little brother. He wore Italian suits and monogrammed shirts and drove a Daimler fitted with a telephone used for very little other than ringing up Harriet with unnecessary messages the moment he was away from the building, like a child with a toy. He also insisted on dragging her along to meetings so that she could take notes of trivial decisions he could just as well have scribbled in a notebook himself. Harvey Jackson believed a secretary was an important adjunct to his image, and that Harriet, cool, blonde and unfailingly efficient, added immeasurably to the impression he made on the world at large.

Harriet rang the typing pool and asked the senior typist to come to her office, then spent an hour indoctrinating an elated Hazel Bishop in the complexities of the job. The girl's coolness towards Harriet actually warmed in her excitement at the prospect of working for Mr Jackson for two whole weeks, and she took the abruptness of her temporary elevation to P.A. level in her stride, with only the expected snide comment about people who could afford to run cars *and* take expensive foreign holidays.

Harriet grinned to herself on the way home as she thought what Hazel's reaction might be if she knew the truth. Her beloved Citröen Deux Chevaux was second-hand and well past its first youth, but even so the cost of the car had ruled out any holiday for Harriet barring a visit to her parents later in the year. She bit her lip as she thought of her parents. A free trip to Portugal was a windfall it would be tricky to explain when she rang them later.

'Are you absolutely positive there are no strings?' demanded her mother. 'Is the man trying to seduce you, Harriet?'

'Mother, you've *met* Mr Jackson. Now is he the type to try anything like that with me?'

'He's a man, isn't he?'

'A *married* man, Mother, with a formidable wife, two children in expensive schools and he belongs to the Rotary club. Men like him don't play around with the hired help.'

Mrs Neil was by no means convinced, and went on at length before changing tack to offer spending money for the holiday. Harriet was touched but refused firmly, well aware how little there was to spare in her parents' household now her father was due to retire from teaching.

'I'm getting holiday money, Mother, thanks just the same. I'll bring you back a plate to hang on the wall.'

Harriet lived in a flat in one of the old Regency houses that were a feature of the town. 'Flat' was rather a grand word for the bed-sitting-room with a kitchen of a cupboard and share of a bathroom, but the room was big, with windows opening on a balcony with a wrought-iron railing, and Harriet loved the bareness and space and went without other things to pay the rent. Not too many other things, she conceded, but she had no need of a hairdresser, was quite clever at making some of her own clothes, ate sparingly and healthily, and her social life was taken care of by the numerous men of her acquaintance who besieged her with invitations. Lately she had begun to see a lot of one in particular, a young man by the name of Jeremy Carter, who had suddenly been seized with the desire to share her flat. He became unexpectedly nasty when his suggestion was turned down, and Harriet was sorry. She liked Jeremy and he was good company and shared a lot of her interests, but as she had no intention of living with anyone, and as he was not prepared to let their relationship 'stagnate' as he put it, he had taken himself off in a temper. Harriet was by no means heartbroken, but the upset was enough to weight the scales in favour of accepting the free holiday. A change of scene would do her good, she decided. She still felt slightly below par after her bout with the virus that had laid most of Harvey Jackson's employees low, and the idea of two weeks in the sun had a definite allure.

Harriet almost regretted her decision next day, which she spent working like a maniac to clear all outstanding mail and anything else Mr Jackson felt essential before her departure. The workload was considerable and not helped by the presence of Hazel at her elbow all day as she laboured to clear her desk. It was gone seven before Harriet felt ready to leave, and on impulse she drove the ten miles to her brother's home near Southam instead of going back to the flat, taking a chance on finding Guy and Delia at home. Her luck was in, fortunately.

'Harriet! You look done in!' Delia Neil pulled her sister-in-law into the warmth of the cottage and shut the door with a bang, diverted from an immediate barrage of questions by the arrival of her husband.

'Hello, Guy,' said Harriet, yawning slightly, and turned to kiss Delia's cheek. 'And hello, Delia, too.'

Young Dr Neil examined his sister's weary face with a professional eye. 'Whatever happened to you?'

'She can tell us in front of the fire over a glass of sherry,' said Delia firmly. 'Can you stay for a meal, love?'

'Yes, please! Thanks, Delia.' Harriet let herself be fussed over and submitted to having her coat unbuttoned and taken off as though she were three, instead of twenty years older than that. 'I had a cold, that's all,' she added.

Guy raised an eyebrow. 'Only one?'

'Well, it was a sort of virus thing and——'

'You didn't take any time off,' finished Delia, who had been a nurse before her marriage, and had red hair and a bracing temperament.

'Stop bullying,' said her husband without heat.

'That boss of hers is such a slave-driver, though—probably wouldn't even notice if she collapsed in front of him!'

'Speak no ill of Horrible Harvey——' began Harriet, then broke off as a large retriever erupted into the room and broke into hysterics at the sight of her. She disappeared under an avalanche of golden fur, protesting wildly.

'Stop that, you idiot dog!' Guy dragged him off with difficulty. 'Where's *he* been?' he asked his wife accusingly. 'Tucked up under our duvet?'

'Ginger feels the cold,' said Delia, unmoved, and returned to her theme. 'What has jolly Mr Jackson been keeping you at today, Harriet? You finished very late if you came straight here from the office.'

'You'll never guess—but I'll explain over dinner. I'm starving.' Harriet drained her glass appreciatively. 'Hope I'm not putting the catering arrangements out, Delia?'

'Of course not. Lamb and rosemary casserole tonight, with a good dollop of red wine—plenty to go round, I promise. Would I be right in thinking you've not had too much of that sort of thing lately?'

'What sort of thing?'

'Home cooking,' said Guy, grinning.

'Oh, I eat, never fear,' Harriet assured them. 'But nothing like the standard of cuisine you get in this house. You don't appreciate your luck, brother dear, having a wife who can both nurse *and* feed you.'

'And sexy with it,' Guy said wickedly, and gave his wife a pat on the bottom as she passed.

'Hands off,' she ordered, laughing, and went to see to dinner.

Harriet jumped up to help but Guy pushed her back in her chair. 'Stay where you are. Delia likes to function alone in the kitchen. Had any medication?' he added casually.

'I took some of those cold capsules in the beginning, but they made me feel a bit strange, sort of hyped up, so I threw them away. In the end I had to go to the doctor.' Harriet pulled a face. 'He gave me antibiotics for my chest and told me to go to bed.'

'And did you?'

'Well, no—I took the pills, but there were so many other people in the firm off sick I felt obliged to soldier on.'

'Idiot!'

Harriet stroked Ginger's glossy coat pensively. 'I've told you before how things are. The girls there still harbour a grudge because I landed the job of Mr Jackson's secretary when I'd only been in the typing pool for a month. Any one of them would be only too pleased to refuse any favour I asked, so I just don't ask any.'

'You should get another job.'

'Easier said than done.' Harriet jumped up as Delia called from the kitchen and followed Guy in eagerly, sniffing at the delicious smell of cooking in the air. As they enjoyed the splendid casserole Harriet told the others about the holiday, giggling at the look of dark suspicion on Delia's face.

'Are you sure you won't find Mr J. in the next bedroom intent on ravishing you as recompense?' asked Delia drily.

'Hardly. You and Mother think alike—she said much the same.'

'They have a point,' said Guy thoughtfully. 'From what you've told us the bloke's not exactly given to charitable gestures much.'

'He doesn't look on me in that light, I assure you,' said Harriet firmly.

'If that's the way you dress at work I'm not surprised.' Delia eyed Harriet's appearance with distaste. 'Why do you screw your hair up like that, for heaven's sake? And that blouse and skirt don't do much for you, either.'

'That's the general idea. And you know what a nuisance my hair is——'

'Nuisance!' snorted Delia. 'I should have such a nuisance. I spend a fortune at the hairdressers.'

'Do you now!' remarked Guy with a grin. 'I never knew that.'

'I meant relatively.' Delia looked enviously at Harriet's hair, which shone guinea-gold under the kitchen light. 'Any woman would sell her soul for hair that colour even if it didn't ripple down her back in a mass of waves, and all she can do is skin it back into a bun!'

'It keeps tidy that way, and makes me look efficient,' said Harriet, and smiled at Guy. 'Remember when Mother made me have it cut short when I was in school? It went into a sort of Afro. At least when it's long I can plait it and pin it out of the way.'

'You must let it down when you go out with Jeremy,

surely. What does he think about the holiday, by the way?'

Harriet accepted a portion of apple pie and gave the others a philosophical smile. 'Jeremy and I are no longer an item. He's taken off in a huff.'

Guy raised his eyebrows. 'Are we allowed to ask why?'

'He asked you to marry him and you turned him down!' said Delia.

'Close. He wanted to move in with me and I turned him down.'

'Why?' asked Delia curiously.

Harriet shook her head at her sister-in-law reprovingly. 'Tut, tut, what a question! I just didn't want to, that's all. Going out together is a bit different from actually living together. Anyway Jeremy seemed to feel I'd misled him and grew distinctly acrimonious, so that was that. Pity, but there are plenty of other blokes around.'

'Perhaps you'll find one in Portugal,' said Guy teasingly.

'Not in the hotel, I shouldn't think. If Harvey Jackson's mother-in-law chose to stay there I hardly think the establishment is likely to be the most swinging place in the Algarve!'

Whatever social life it offered the Hotel Miramar proved to be very picturesque to look at, at least, and Harriet's spirits rose when she stepped off the coach after the journey from Faro airport. The other passengers were all in her parents' age-group, which was only what she had expected, nevertheless she felt a little dampened to find no one at all of her own age and turned her attention to the hotel by way of consolation. It was white and Moorish in atmosphere, long and cool-looking in the bright sunlight, and no more than five storeys high, a fact which met with Harriet's warm approval. Inside the building the foyer was bustling with a flood of new arrivals, and she gazed about her with interest as she waited in line at the reception desk where a team of receptionists were working at top speed to welcome the influx of guests, allot keys and send bell-boys in various directions with luggage. The foyer was cool, despite the crowd, and very spacious, with some walls decorated with blue and white tiles, others with glass cases displaying souvenirs and local crafts, and her room, when she finally reached it, was surprisingly large, with full-length windows opening on a verandah that gave a panoramic view of the spectacular beach. Full marks to Mr Jackson's mother-in-law, poor soul, thought Harriet, and gave the boy who carried her bags a generous tip before succumbing to the lure of the comfortable-looking bed as she stretched out full length with a sigh.

When she woke with a start some time later she found the room full of shadows, and became instantly aware of how hungry she was. The meal on the plane was a thing of the past and she wanted whatever dinner the Hotel Miramar was able to provide, and as quickly as possible. She showered quickly, then brushed her glittering mane of hair before plaiting it into a thick braid which she coiled at the nape of her neck. She took time for the merest minimum of make-up before pulling on a long-waisted dress in slate-blue cotton jersey printed in white, and pulled a face at her reflection in the mirror. The material was uncrushable, but it was last year's summer dress, and pre-virus there had been a lot more of Harriet inside it than at the moment. She shrugged and picked up her bag as she left the room. A couple of weeks handed to her on a plate, with nothing to do but eat and loll about in the sun, would no doubt remedy the deficit. Going down in the lift she experienced a slight qualm, and hoped her table in the dining-room would be fairly near the door, as she had no fancy to march alone down a ballroom-sized restaurant. Happily the suave, maroon-jacketed head-waiter at the door led her to a small table against the back wall where she had a view of the entire glass-fronted room without having to pass too many tables to reach it.

People were milling about all over the place to her

surprise. Sunday evening, she was informed, in surprisingly good English, was cold buffet night. The *senhora* would be served with soup by a waiter, but after that she would kindly help herself from the enormous array of cold dishes on the long table in the middle of the room. Harriet felt a lot better. The atmosphere was more informal than expected, and the other guests crowded round the central buffet table were more interested in the array of food than remarking on a girl dining alone. And there was no reason why they should, she told herself flatly. Spending a holiday alone was hardly a world-shattering course of action; just something she herself had never done before. She was used to eating out with a mixed crowd, or alone with a male escort, and previous holidays had been spent with first the family, then friends. Until this moment she had never thought about feeling conspicuous, which she did, however much she told herself not to be so stupid.

She ate her meal rapidly and left the dining-room to go in search of coffee in the bar. She sat on a comfortable couch near the windows and drank the coffee the shy, good-looking young waiter brought, recklessly ordering a brandy to mitigate the dismay she felt. Her surprise over Harvey Jackson's free holiday had entirely blinded her to the fact that she might feel out of place in a hotel which at first glance seemed to be populated entirely by British family units of varying kinds. The dining-room had been full of elderly and middle-aged couples, young couples, even ladies in pairs, but no one, it seemed, was alone like herself. Pensively she sipped the cognac and wondered how Mr Jackson's mother-in-law would have fared. Harriet sighed a little and resolved to make the best of it. She was here for two weeks and she would just have to enjoy herself the best way she could; do some shopping, read a lot, go on trips and see as much of her surroundings as possible. Her knowledge of Portugal was confined to something vague about Prince Henry the Navigator and port wine, and the Algarve to a mental picture of sunflowers and windmills and miles of golden beach, so now she had a good opportunity to improve on it.

She woke very early next morning and went to stand on the balcony to look at the view in the pale gold light of dawn. By craning her neck to look landward she could just catch sight of the rather ramshackle charm of Praia do Ceu, which appeared to be just a fairly sleepy little fishing village, with no other hotels in view. Ahead of her lay the great sweep of the beach. The golden symmetry of the sand was broken at intervals by the fantasy shapes sculptured from the sand-stone cliffs by the sea, where fishing boats bobbed peacefully on the glittering waves, looking for all the world as though their only function was to provide the perfect picture for the tourists' cameras. Harriet breathed in deeply in sheer delight, her misgivings of the evening before firmly routed, and she decided to take a walk. Quickly she pulled on white cotton jeans and an emerald sweatshirt, and tied a green scarf over her hair before going down in the lift and across the foyer, smiling at the army of women dusting and polishing there as she went out into the blue and gold morning.

She walked briskly along the narrow pavement lining the seaward side of the road, where a narrow strip of ornamental garden boasted palms and geraniums in profusion. On the other side houses and small apartment buildings vied with each other in varying pastel colours, giving way at one point to a tiny square dominated by a sugar-pink church before the road narrowed and led her to the heart of Praia do Ceu. This was the harbour where the fishing boats set off to catch the abundant fish of the beautiful Algarve coast. She came to a quay with a minuscule chapel topped by a bell tower, and paused near it to lean against the sea wall and watch the activity. In the distance she could see the beginnings of a new marina in construction, dazzling in its whiteness in the early sunshine, but below her countless boats were drawn

up on the sand and fishing nets were spread out
everywhere she looked. Even though it was early the
place was alive with people. The market was already in
full swing, selling fresh vegetables and newly baked
bread, the smell of which was so delicious Harriet's
stomach rumbled, and she wished she had brought some
money with her. She turned away, pushing her sunglasses
more firmly on her nose as she watched the colourful
scene below, when suddenly a little eddying breeze
caught the scarf she was wearing and lifted it clean off
her head to deposit it a short distance away at the feet of a
man crouched mending one of the boats. He grinned at
the feminine trifle and stood up with it in his hand,
looking round for the owner. Harriet's hair, streaming
loose without the scarf, whipped in a bright gold mass
across her face, and she brushed it away impatiently as
she ran down to the sand to claim her scarf. The man
holding it stayed where he was, staring as she hurried
towards him, and Harriet smiled at him diffidently. He
was taller than the other Portuguese men she'd seen so
far, but just as dark, with thick black curling hair and
heavy straight brows in a very good-looking, grave face.
The smell of paint and fish was strong as Harriet reached
him and she felt awkward, wondering if he spoke any
English. He was barefoot and very shabby. His dark blue
jersey had a hole in the elbow and his canvas trousers
were salt-stained and daubed with paint. He held her
scarf between the tips of his thumb and forefinger as he
went on looking at her in silence.

'That's my scarf,' Harriet ventured awkwardly.
'Thank you for rescuing it.'

'De nada, senhora,' he answered, and held it out to her,
still watching her closely from eyes narrowed against the
sun.

Harriet took the scarf gingerly and backed away.
'Well—thank you again.'

The man inclined his head slightly, but said nothing
more, and she turned away, tying the scarf securely in

place again, wishing she had taken the time to braid her hair as usual before coming out. The fisherman had stared at it as though he'd never seen anything like it before, which was nonsense. The place had to be thick with tourists for the best part of the year, and plenty of them would be blonde. She shrugged and went quickly back to the hotel. She spent five minutes in her room plaiting her hair and collecting her bag, then went down to buy a morning paper from the shop in the foyer, and read it while she had toast and coffee in the almost empty dining-room. Afterwards Harriet went to find a sunbed on the terrace above the pool. She stripped off her jeans and sweatshirt to the green seersucker bikini underneath, anointing herself liberally with sun-cream before settling down to read the paperback novel bought at the airport the day before. As the morning wore on the sunbeds near her gradually filled, mainly with older people, though she could see several younger couples on the terrace below watching over children frolicking in the pool, which was cleverly built among the natural rock to look like a work of nature rather than the skill of the architect.

Harriet retreated under the umbrella's shelter by mid-morning, taking care not to burn her skin, which had a creamy pallor that took time to take on any colour from the sun. She sighed and wrinkled her nose at the words on the page in front of her, frankly admitting to herself that she was a little bit bored, and this while she was still a little tired. Heaven help her when she was running on all cylinders again! She thought wistfully of childhood holidays with Guy and her parents, the holiday in Yugoslavia with her friend Anna the year they left school—wonderful! Since then it had been business college, then work, and the only real holiday had been a memorable, hilarious skiing trip to Val d'Isère with a group of friends one Easter. And now this holiday to Portugal, which was the first one on her own, and in spite of the comfortable hotel and spectacular location she was not enjoying herself as much as expected so far. The most interesting male encountered up to now was the strong, silent fisherman on the beach, and even apart from the language barrier he hadn't seemed nearly as taken with her as she was with him, anyway, which was sad. Harriet grinned. The man probably had a wife and a houseful of children. She turned over on her stomach and stared out to sea. Pity Mr Jackson's mother-in-law hadn't fancied one of those touring holidays—the 'It's Tuesday so it must be Rome' variety. Nevertheless, thought Harriet, it was hardly the thing to look a gift-horse in the mouth, and she should be grateful. It was just that loneliness was something she had never anticipated. She adored living alone, but this, somehow, was different.

She gave herself a mental shake. It was less than a day since her arrival—hardly time to start feeling sorry for herself. The cure was to do something about it. This afternoon she would wander down to the village again, armed with money this time, and later on the courier was due at the Miramar to take bookings for trips and give whatever help and advice was needed, and she would make sure she booked up for as many excursions as possible. Harriet felt better at once, and ordered coffee and sandwiches from the poolside bar, lingering with her book afterwards until late in the afternoon. After changing into a cotton skirt and T-shirt she left the hotel to stroll down to the village to explore the cobbled square with the twin-towered pink church, and found several shops tucked away behind it. There were dark, cool little bars with marble-topped counters, a window full of embroidered linens, and to her surprise a little arcade, lined with shops selling leather goods, shoes, even furniture, with the inevitable *supermercado* at the end full of expensive imported delicacies and inexpensive local products, including wine. On her way back to the little *praça* Harriet noticed a small shop tucked away in a corner, where a young girl sat painting china plates. She was pretty, with black hair hanging down her back, and she worked with great speed and dexterity, the floor space around her stool covered with plates recently painted and set out to dry before firing.

The finished products hanging on the walls were painted with local scenes; animals, sunflowers, windmills, the inevitable good-luck cockerel of Portugal, all the things most likely to catch the tourist fancy, but executed with a delicacy lacking in the usual run-of-the-mill souvenirs. One thing, in particular, caught Harriet's eye, more vivid than the rest, and very different. It was a great cornucopia of fruits and vegetables: oranges, lemons, peppers, beans, melons and onions spilling in an exuberant cascade of colour. Harriet could just picture it on the high walls of her room in Leamington.

'Hello,' she said quietly, careful not to startle the girl from her concentration.

The young artist looked up with a smile. 'Hello.'

Harriet gestured towards the ceramic fruit. 'How much, please?'

The girl named a sum in escudos, and after a quick calculation Harriet was surprised to find it so reasonable, particularly an article of such quality. She sighed. The price was feasible, but the size was not. Getting it home on the plane was out of the question. 'Yours?' she asked.

The girl nodded smiling. 'You like?'

'Oh, I do, very much indeed.' Harriet smiled ruefully. 'But I came by aeroplane——'

'*Compreendo.* Is too large. *Que pena!*' The girl smiled again sympathetically, but made no effort to suggest something else as substitute.

'May I look at some plates?' Harriet was determined to buy something painted by the girl.

'*Poisè.* Of course.' The girl resumed painting as Harriet edged her way gingerly round the little shop, careful to avoid the plates drying on the floor as she examined others on the walls. So many appealed to her she had difficulty in choosing, but finally settled for two different views of Praia do Ceu, one for her mother and the other for Delia. As she paid for them she gave a last look at the ceramic fruit again, miming her regret to the girl before leaving. As she emerged into the sunshine of the square she hesitated, casting a look towards the harbour, then laughed at herself and turned briskly back to the hotel, putting thoughts of handsome Portuguese fishermen firmly from her mind.

When she arrived the courier was already installed in the main lounge, and she went straight in to see him before going upstairs with her spoils. He was a young local man, very efficient and pleasant, and spoke English colloquial enough to laugh and joke with the people waiting to avail themselves of his services. After only a short wait Harriet was booked on the next overnight trip to Lisbon, a shorter one to Lagos and Sagres, which Manoel told her was known as '*O fim do mundo*', world's end. He also persuaded her to a further day trip to Albufeira.

'One seat only?' he enquired, eyes dancing.

'Afraid so,' said Harriet with a sigh.

Upstairs in her room she wrote some postcards, then ran a bath and lay in it as long as possible, spinning out the time until it was near the dinner hour. The evening was a little chillier than she had expected and she was glad of the long, drop-shouldered sleeves of her forest-green shirt-dress as she got ready. She fastened a wide suede belt round her hips, added a long string of amber beads, and noted with approval that her skin had already taken on a faint glow from its first dose of Algarvean sun. In spite of her dawdling it was still a little early for dinner, so she went down to the cocktail bar and ordered a Martini from the same waiter, who greeted her with a friendly smile this time. Tonight she was early enough to watch the sunset from her vantage point near the window, and gazed, fascinated, as the sun poured molten radiance over the brilliant scarlets and pinks of the geraniums and mesembryanthemums in the terraced hotel gardens. The bar was almost empty, everyone else presumably getting ready for dinner or already consuming it, and Harriet stared absently at the view, wondering how Mr Jackson was getting on with Hazel Bishop, and speculating, not for the first time, on the strange impulse which had moved him to the unprecedented burst of generosity.

When Harriet finally made a move to go into dinner she found the table next to hers occupied by a middle-aged couple and a younger pair, obviously both husbands and wives. They all smiled and said good evening in friendly fashion as she sat down, and Harriet smiled back, turning her attention to the menu with a little glow. She had finished her tomato juice and was eating the sole which followed when she noticed a slight stir in the centre of the room as the proprietor of the hotel came in with several members of his family to take possession of the large table kept reserved for them. Harriet almost choked on a mouthful of fish as she recognised the man with them. It was her fisherman, transformed completely by the elegance of the pale grey suit he was wearing. The quality of it was very obvious, even at a distance, and Harriet's cheeks burned as she returned her eyes to her plate and kept them there, hoping she would go unnoticed. The waiter removed her fish and replaced it with steak innocent of garlic, to Harriet's surprise. Deference to the British palate, she thought with amusement, but found her enthusiasm for her dinner had waned anyway since seeing the stranger from the beach. She felt oddly put out at being so taken in by his appearance earlier, and thanked her lucky stars she hadn't put her foot in it by trying to talk to him, or worse, giving him a tip for rescuing her scarf. She winced at the thought and wondered who he was. It seemed likely he was a relative of the proprietor, by the easy way he was chatting with his companions when she risked a look in his direction. She regretted it instantly as his eyes caught and held hers, and with deliberation he raised his wineglass in silent toast.

Harriet flushed and turned away, refusing the blandishments of the young waiter with the dessert trolley in her haste to get away. The foursome at the next table were leaving as she passed, and introduced themselves as the Armstrongs, asking her if she were alone and if she would care to have coffee with them. Harriet was delighted, and kept her eyes away from the centre table as she accompanied the Armstrongs to the main lounge, where a pianist was playing Hoagy Carmichael melodies while waiters circulated with coffee and liqueurs. Her companions were Dora and George Armstrong, their son Tony and his wife Jane. They were cheerful, pleasant people, Jane only a little older than Harriet and very dark and vivacious in contrast to her slim, fair-haired young husband. The other two hardly looked old enough to be the parents of Tony, and Harriet told them so with sincerity.

'Just for that I'll buy you a brandy,' said George Armstrong, beaming, and the others laughed.

'You've made a friend for life,' teased his son. 'After hearing that he'll beat me into the dust on the golf- course tomorrow!'

This was their third holiday in the Algarve, Jane explained, and they now had a formula that worked very well. The men played golf on alternate days and did whatever their wives organised for them on the others.

'Shopping, if we bully them enough,' said Dora with a twinkle.

The Armstrongs were kind, undemanding company and the time passed quickly as they waited for the folk-dancers who were due to perform there later.

'We saw flamenco stuff in Spain,' said Tony, 'but the dancing they do here is quite a contrast.'

'Stuff!' said Jane despairingly. 'How can you describe those gorgeous, graceful creatures and wonderful guitar music as "stuff"!'

'None of you youngsters can dance, anyway,' said Mr Armstrong. 'All that jerking about on your own—I like to get to grips with a woman myself.'

He was saved from a lecture from his wife by the arrival of the troupe of dancers, who were teenagers, to Harriet's surprise, except for the musicians. One man played an accordion, another a triangle, and two older men just clapped in time to the music as the dancers stamped and trotted in a naïve, lively rhythm far removed from the sensual hauteur of the flamenco. These youngsters danced in pairs, the girls in heavy braided skirts which flew up to reveal frilled bloomers and thick white knitted stockings, and the young men in dark trousers and waistcoats with round black felt hats on their heads. They ran and stamped and clapped, the steps changing with the music, tiring Harriet just to watch their enthusiasm and energy. Suddenly one youth darted from the dance floor and caught Jane by the hand, pulling her into the dance while his partner seized one of the watching men.

Harriet and the Armstrongs laughed uproariously at Jane's mock-anguish, then to her horror Harriet was the next victim, hauled without ceremony on to the packed floor. On her mettle to keep up with her partner, Harriet matched him step for step, whirling with hands high above her head, or linking them with his as they tore round the floor in time to the music, which wickedly grew faster and faster as the dancers whirled and the holidaymakers tried to keep up the pace. Spots began to flicker in front of her eyes and her gasps for breath hurt her chest, to her consternation. I'm going to make an exhibition of myself, she thought, with the calm of the desperate. I shall fall on the floor and everyone will pile in a heap on top of me. Then the lights began to blur and her calm turned to sheer panic the instant before very different, cool hands took hers and pulled her away from the crowd, guiding her swiftly outside to the terrace. The fresh air felt wonderful on her face as the spots receded, her breathing slowed and she collected herself sufficiently to push away the hair that had tumbled from its loose knot and turn to thank her rescuer. The words stuck in her throat as she stared at the tall man standing close, as if ready to catch her. With a feeling of inevitability she recognised her mysterious fisherman, only this time he was smiling down at her in a way that affected her much-tried respiratory system as badly as the energetic antics of the folk dance.

'I—I don't even know how to say "thank you" in Portuguese,' she said and pushed at her unruly hair.

'You say "*obrigado*",' he informed her, the English words as accentless as her own.

'You're not Portuguese?' she asked, startled.

Her rescuer shook his head. 'I'm almost as British as you are.'

'Almost?'

'My grandmother was Portuguese.' He leaned closer to examine her face in the dim light. 'Are you feeling better now?'

Harriet thought this over. 'Yes—yes, I am.' She smiled at him ruefully. 'I'm in your debt.'

'*De nada, senhora*.' His smile mocked her and Harriet's cheeks grew warm as she thought of the little early morning encounter.

'How did you know I felt odd?' she asked curiously.

'I was watching you as you danced.' His voice was attractive, deep and slightly harsh. 'You suddenly changed colour—your face looked almost green against that noticeable hair as it came loose. I thought you were going to faint.'

'So did I—for a moment I was convinced I was about to cause a pile-up on the dance-floor.' She held out her hand. 'Thank you very much for rescuing me. I'd better go in again, or my companions will be wondering what's happened to me.'

He took her hand in his, which was surprisingly hard and calloused. 'Won't you tell me your name?'

'Neil. Harriet Neil.'

'Richard Livesey. I'm very happy to meet you, Miss Neil.'

His eyes held hers for a long moment in silence while Harriet tried in vain to think of something graceful to say, then he dropped her hand abruptly as Jane came hurrying through the door with Tony hard on her heels.

'Harriet, are you all right? Dora said——' She stopped short at the sight of the tall man with Harriet. 'Oh, I'm sorry—I didn't realise——'

'This is the good Samaritan who rescued me from making an exhibition of myself in there.' Harriet waved a hand airily towards the door. 'Jane, Tony, this is Richard Livesey. Mr Livesey, Mr and Mrs Armstrong.' She felt an odd need for formality, and stood by in silence while the dark, undeniably attractive Mr Livesey was charm itself to the young couple. They were patently very impressed and invited him to have a drink with their parents.

'That's very kind of you, but I'm staying with friends in the Vale do Centianes, which means a drive home, and Portuguese views on drinking and driving are very much the same as in England, so I'll hold you to that drink another time.' With an almost formal little bow in Harriet's direction and a smile for the other two Richard Livesey took his leave and disappeared into the darkness of the hotel garden, in the direction of the car park.

'Are you all right now, Harriet?' asked Tony sympathetically.

Harriet turned rather blank eyes on him. 'Yes—yes, I'm fine. I just felt a bit dizzy, that's all, and Mr Livesey brought me out here before any harm was done.'

'Nice work if you can get it,' said Jane with a grin. 'Did your hair fall down before you came out or afterwards?'

Harriet laughed and tried to tidy the tumbling mass. 'Before! I should have plaited it as usual, but I wasn't expecting a dance marathon like that.'

'It's very spectacular hair. Your Mr Livesey couldn't take his eyes off it,' said Jane enviously.

'I get fed up with it myself—people tend to forget a brain exists underneath it if I leave my crowning glory to its own devices. And he's not my Mr Livesey!' added Harriet, as they went in to join the others.

Despite her emphatic words she kept seeing Richard Livesey's strong-featured face in her mind as she lay in bed later listening to the soft boom of the surf on the beach below. She clasped her hands behind her head, remembering the unexpected roughness of his fingers, and wondered what he did for a living, if he were married—— At the last her mind put on the brakes and Harriet gave herself a stringent little lecture. Mr Jackson's gift of a holiday had been miracle enough; it was expecting rather a lot to hope for a romantic interlude as well.

CHAPTER TWO

HARRIET felt utterly different when she woke next morning. The doubts and ennui of the day before had vanished like a bad dream, and she sparkled with energy, her spirits fizzing inside her like champagne. Without analysing the reasons for the change she put on a brief white bikini, added pink shorts and shirt, threw her usual clutter of impedimenta into her large beach-bag and went in search of breakfast. She ordered fried eggs, crisp smoked bacon with tomatoes and mushrooms and followed it up with toast and marmalade, and was on her second cup of coffee when the Armstrong ladies arrived at the next table.

'It's plain to see you're fully recovered this morning,' said Dora, smiling. 'The men are golfing and Jane and I intend to loaf about in the sun with the morning papers. Would you care to join us or do you have other plans?'

Harriet had no plans at all and was only too happy to

lie on a sunbed near the pool and indulge in some unaccustomed feminine chatter, a luxury she rarely enjoyed unless she went home for a weekend or spent an hour with Delia. It was pleasantly relaxing, and a couple of hours went past quickly. The three of them were drinking coffee when a waiter came up to tell Harriet she was wanted on the telephone. Mystified and rather anxious, she excused herself, wondering if something were wrong at home as she hurried to the alcove indicated by one of the pretty, courteous receptionists.

'Harriet Neil,' she said cautiously into the handset.

'Good morning,' answered a deep voice, and Harriet's heart did a flip in her chest. 'Richard Livesey here, Miss Neil. I called to ask how you are after your little misadventure last night.'

'That's very kind of you, Mr Livesey. I'm very well indeed today, thank you.'

'Well enough to have dinner with me tonight?'

Harriet's athletic heart gave another lurch, and she bit her lip. 'I don't quite know how to answer that,' she said honestly

'What's wrong with "yes"?' He sounded amused.

'I really don't think——' she began, but he interrupted.

'If you want references José Oliveira, the hotel proprietor, will vouch for me. I'm perfectly respectable, I swear.'

Harriet's every instinct was to shout 'yes, please' into the telephone, but some contrary shred of caution held her back. 'It's very kind of you, Mr Livesey, but I don't feel I can accept.' And with great care she replaced the receiver.

Jane and Dora looked anxious as Harriet flopped down again beside them. 'Nothing wrong, I hope?' asked Jane.

'No—it was a polite enquiry about my health from the man who extricated me from the revels last night.'

There were knowing looks from the Armstrongs, but

Harriet just smiled and settled down to enjoy the sun. After a sandwich lunch Dora decided to have a nap in her room and left the two girls together. In the shade of the umbrella they both dozed for a while, then Harriet stirred and saw the pool was empty.

'Come on, Jane, let's get in the water before all the teenies come back from their siestas.'

The two girls stayed in the water until they tired of racing each other along the length of the pool. Afterwards, as they were towelling themselves dry, Jane eyed Harriet speculatively.

'Did tall, dark and handsome really only ask about your health this morning? Tell me to shut up and mind my own business if you like.'

Harriet laughed as she freed her hair from its braid to dry. 'Well, now you mention it, Mr Livesey did throw in an invitation to dinner while he was at it.'

'Really?' Jane's eyes sparkled as she towelled her short dark curls. 'Where's he taking you?'

'He's not taking me anywhere. I said thanks, but no, thanks.'

'You're joking!'

'I'm not.'

'Why, Harriet? Didn't you *want* to go?'

'You bet I did,' said Harriet candidly, and combed her fingers through her wet hair, sighing. 'My instinct was to say yes, but I just couldn't somehow. Too pat, too easy. You know what he must have in mind—fun-loving lady tourist on holiday alone, on the look-out for a spot of excitement to liven things up. It seemed a pity to let Mr Livesey proceed further along the wrong lines, that's all.'

Jane looked frankly doubtful. 'He *is* rather gorgeous, though. I only met him for a moment, but he's a mature, sophisticated man by the look of him, not some callow lout on the prowl. I think you should have accepted.'

'Too late now.' Harriet smoothed more suntan cream over her long legs. 'I just didn't feel like chancing my arm with a stranger at the drop of a hat—always supposing it was my arm he was interested in, of course.'

Jane grinned, and cast a glance at the curves of the figure lounging beside her. 'I expect he noticed the rest, if he's normal—and I'd bet my boots he *was* normal, wouldn't you?'

'Exactly. So I said no. I get annoyed when men get preoccupied with the packaging. He was probably so busy staring at my wretched hair he never noticed there's a reasonably intelligent female that goes with it.'

'You haven't given the man a chance!'

'We're just ships that pass in the night, Jane—or perhaps I mean fishing boats.'

'What—oh, there's Tony. The golfers have returned.' Jane jumped up, smiling at her sunburned husband, who came with an invitation to tea in the lounge, as both men had had enough sun. Harriet declined, grateful for the offer, but preferring to remain alone in the warm sunshine with a tray of tea from the poolside bar. Her novel had begun to grip her, and she became so engrossed in it she failed to notice that eventually she was the only occupant of the terrace, even the waiters deserting it for their evening duties as the sun sank lower in the sky. Harriet read on and on, oblivious to her sudden lack of company, and only stirred when a cool breeze sprang up. She shivered a little and sat up to put on her shirt, jerking bolt upright with a gasp as she saw Richard Livesey sitting motionless on the end of Jane's sunbed. She scrambled for her shirt, pushing her tangle of damp, untidy hair behind her ears.

'How long have you been there?' she demanded resentfully, too startled for a polite greeting.

'Only a minute or two.' Richard looked at her steadily as she buttoned up her shirt hurriedly and took a look round the deserted terrace. He was dressed only a little more respectably than the morning before in the same disreputable jeans, but now there were espadrilles on the bare brown feet, and instead of the ragged jersey a white sweatshirt drew attention to a very muscular pair of shoulders.

'You could have said something,' muttered Harriet.

'Your concentration was so intense I hadn't the temerity to interrupt.'

She eyed him suspiciously. 'Why are you here?'

'To persuade you to change your mind.' There was challenge in his eyes, which were a dark blue instead of the black Harriet had expected. 'I was curious to know just why you wouldn't dine with me,' he added.

'Why should you want me to?'

A slow smile set his face alight, and she blinked. Odd, she thought irrelevantly, how a mere facial distortion can change a man's appearance. In repose Richard Livesey's face had an almost classic regularity, with straight black brows and a rather long, patrician nose above a wide mouth with a thin curving upper lip almost at odds with the sensual curve of the lower one. But when he smiled one half of his face seemed to function independently of the other, one eye closing more than its twin, accentuating the fan of laughter-lines at the corners, and one half of his mouth lifted higher than the other in a crooked grin of immense charm. Harriet recalled herself hurriedly as her unexpected visitor said something with a patience that suggested he was repeating it.

'I said I thought it was obvious,' he said. 'We're both here in the Algarve alone—at least I assume you are alone. What harm can there be in spending a little time together? I know the area quite well, in case it's new to you.' He leaned forward a little. 'What exactly do you object to about me?'

Harriet began to busy herself with packing her belongings into her bag. 'Nothing. I'm just suspicious, I suppose. Yesterday morning I thought you were just Pedro the fisherman, then last night you turn up as the guest of the hotel proprietor, which was confusing, for a start. Then you made rather a point of pursuing the acquaintance, so I assumed you were on the make; in pursuit of a little uncomplicated dalliance with a lonely, and suitably grateful, tourist.'

Richard Livesey drew back, his eyes suddenly cold. 'You're mistaken. At the risk of sounding big-headed I might add that if sexual diversion were my object I'm not obliged to seek it from the lady tourists who frequent José Oliveira's hotel.'

Harriet looked at him steadily for a moment, then got up, shrugging apologetically. 'If I was wrong I apologise. But from past experience I've found men judge by the icing rather than the basic ingredients of the cake.'

Richard rose to his feet and stood looking down at her with wry amusement. 'In your case, Miss Neil, you must admit a mere male can be forgiven for it; the icing is quite extraordinarily attractive!'

Harriet, accustomed to compliments all her life, flushed to the roots of her hair and the man watching her stared, fascinated, as the colour rose from the opening of her shirt to her hair, like claret spilt in a bowl of cream.

'It's time I went in,' she said, embarrassed, but the man barred her way.

'Change your mind—please,' he said, so emphatically her eyes flew to meet his, startled. 'Please,' he repeated quietly, something in the expression of his blue eyes making her capitulate with a suddenness that surprised herself as much as Richard Livesey.

'Where did you intend dining?' she asked casually.

'At a restaurant near the beach on the far side of the village. The fish there is superb.' He stood aside to let her pass, then walked with her along the terrace to the back entrance of the hotel foyer.

'Oh, very well then,' said Harriet. 'About eight-thirty—I'll wait for you here in the foyer.'

He paused at the big glass doors, looking down at her curiously. 'What made you change your mind?'

She gave him a sudden wicked grin, her eyes dancing in a way that made his own flicker in surprise. 'I just can't resist fish!'

Richard Livesey remained outside on the terrace as the graceful, bright-haired girl left him to go inside the hotel, a blank, frowning look on his face that would have puzzled Harriet had she turned to see it.

She went into the lift without a backward glance, however, intent on spending the next couple of hours in grooming herself to the very highest pinnacle of elegance she could achieve, spurred on by the memory of Richard Livesey's faultless appearance of the night before. There was no point in denying that she felt excited. As she lay in the bath she fairly tingled with anticipation, and her hair crackled as she dried it afterwards, as though she were generating extra life through the burnished strands. She whistled cheerfully, deciding to enjoy her evening to the full now her pride had been salvaged by refusing Richard's invitation the first time round. She grinned at herself in the mirror, frankly admitting how flattering it was to have such an attractive man pursue her with such persistence. Richard Livesey was far and away the most exciting man she had ever met, and in retrospect it seemed rather feeble to pass up a pleasant evening with him just because he was a passing ship, as she'd said to Jane.

Humming off-key, she gave herself a manicure and then applied a careful minimum of make-up to a face glowing very satisfactorily from the sun. She slid into the white satin teddy that was all the underwear necessary under a lined white silk dress she had made herself in a clever copy of a Benny Ong model. Sleeveless and simple, it had a hip-length jacket in amber and white stripes, and she had bought plain white kid pumps to go with it. Small gold studs in her ears, her hair wound into a casual, heavy knot on the crown of her head, and Harriet felt ready to take on the world, let alone Richard Livesey. When she emerged from the lift the Armstrongs were crossing the foyer *en route* to the dining-room, and rather sheepishly Harriet was able to explain her absence from the dinner table, laughing at the storm of teasing she had to endure from all sides when she mentioned Richard's visit to the terrace earlier.

'Wore you down in the end, did he?' Jane winked. 'Must be keen!'

'You watch your step, young lady,' advised George Armstrong. 'Remember he's a stranger, and you look very tempting indeed this evening—so don't let him keep you out too late.'

'Don't listen to him,' put in Tony, smiling. 'Dance all night if you feel like it.'

'My escort mentioned something about fish—not dancing!'

'Fish!' Jane rolled her eyes. 'Surely he can do better than that. We'll expect a full report tomorrow, of course!'

After they left her Harriet sat on one of the velvet sofas in the foyer, wishing she had taken longer to dress. It seemed to smack of over-enthusiasm to be ready and waiting well before time. It was only a minute or two, however, before the tall figure she was watching for appeared through the revolving door with almost ten minutes to spare, looking impressive in black linen trousers, snowy shirt and a silver-grey jacket. Richard strode towards her, hand outstretched, and Harriet rose automatically, letting him clasp her own.

'A pearl without price, a punctual woman,' he said with a gleam of white teeth. 'I hope you're suitably impressed by the speed with which I've managed to get back here at the stipulated hour."

'I might be even more impressed if I knew exactly how far you had to go,' she remarked pertly.

He laughed. 'Honesty forces me to own up to only a few kilometres, I'm afraid.'

'But honesty's always the best policy, Mr Livesey!' Harriet smiled up at him as he led her towards the door, her eyebrows lifting a little as she fancied she saw an odd flicker in the dark-blue eyes.

'Is that your own personal code for living?' he asked.

Harriet looked at him thoughtfully and nodded. 'Yes, it is.'

Richard appeared to shrug off his moment of gravity as they walked to the white Mercedes parked outside. 'You look very beautiful this evening—if I'm allowed to make such a frivolous comment.'

'Oh yes! One likes one's efforts to be appreciated.'

He helped her into the car with care, then went round to get in himself, pausing to look at her in a way she found rather unnerving.

'What is it?' she asked uneasily.

'I was just thinking you looked just as beautiful earlier with your hair all over the place and your face as nature made it.'

Harriet's eyes dropped and she fiddled with the seatbelt. 'If that was a compliment, thank you.'

'It was the truth,' he said unanswerably, and started the car.

The distance to the restaurant was so short Harriet looked at her companion with laughing reproach as they drew up in a cobbled courtyard near the beach. The building was hung with pots of geraniums and inside had a dining-room with windows overlooking the sea and the firefly lights of the fishing-boats anchored off-shore. A waiter led them to a table near one of the windows, and Harriet sat down, looking about her at the crowded restaurant with unconcealed pleasure. At the far end of the room a wrought-iron screen gave a view of a dark-skinned chef presiding over an open charcoal grill, and there was a wonderful atmosphere of warmth and congeniality in the room that appealed to her enormously.

'This is lovely,' she said, and watched as the waiter produced a basket of crusty bread, a dish of butter and another of curd cheese, arranging them with ceremony on the snowy starched cloth while her host conferred with the wine waiter.

'It's not a sophisticated place,' Richard informed her

when they were alone, 'but the fish one eats was
swimming out there this morning, there's no synthetic
music to drown conversation, and the service is pleasant.
It won't be very swift, of course, but from my point of
view that's a definite advantage—gives me more time
with such a delightful companion.'

Harriet eyed him quizzically. 'You might become
bored with my company before you've finished your first
course. After all, you hardly know me.'

'True.' Richard smiled. 'But I trust good manners, if
nothing else, would insist I allowed you to finish your
dinner before I rushed you back to the Miramar—
Harriet?

There was a slight question in his voice as he used her
first name for the first time.

'*Touché*, Richard,' she countered, answering his
question, then turned her attention to the enormous
menu. 'Now how about giving me a hand with this lot; I
warn you I'm hungry.'

'I'm pleased to hear it—I loathe watching a woman
pick at her food.' He leaned close to translate the various
dishes and Harriet found concentration difficult, aston-
ished to find her whole body reacting to the brush of his
shoulder against hers and the casual touch of his hand as
he turned the pages of the menu.

She pulled herself together hurriedly. It was a new
experience to find herself so responsive to a man's
physical presence, and she wasn't at all sure she liked it.
With an effort she applied herself to Richard's description of an endless list of dishes, and after much discussion
agreed to share a *calderada*.

'Fish stew, in other words,' said Richard with a grin.

This was a very mundane description for the delicious
concoction of fresh tomatoes, onions, potatoes and
succulent bits of every kind of fish available, all cooked
together with a little oil, garlic and a type of paprika
known locally as *colorau*. It arrived steaming in a copper

pot and Harriet sniffed ecstatically at the heavenly aroma.

'Good thing I opted out of a first course,' she remarked as the waiter ladled a generous serving on to her plate. The dish was utterly delicious, she found, peppery, but not aggressively so, and full of morsels of lobster, sole, hake and mackerel, shrimps, prawns, clams and another delicacy she found hard to identify.

'Lamprey,' said Richard, his face alight with amusement at her frank enjoyment of the meal. 'You approve, I take it?'

'Out of this world,' she said briefly, and concentrated on her meal until at last she laid down her knife and fork with a sigh. 'That was delectable—I couldn't eat another thing.'

Richard leaned forward to fill her wineglass. 'Surely you can find room for one of the local *doces*?'

'What are they?'

'Sweetmeats made with egg yolks and sugar and almonds, endless varieties. Perhaps you'd care to try one of the *barrigas de freiras*?' Something in the gleam in his eyes alerted Harriet.

'Translate,' she instructed.

'Nuns' tummies,' he said promptly.

She choked on her wine with a gurgle. 'Nuns' tummies! You, Mr Livesey, are pulling my leg!'

'A tempting thought, but I assure you I'm not.'

They laughed together companionably and finished the wine, then lingered over coffee after Harriet refused the dessert, despite its exotic name. She eyed him speculatively over her coffee-cup.

'Why were you mending a fishing-boat yesterday?' she asked bluntly. 'Do you go out fishing?'

'No. I was just lending a hand with a repair. I like messing about in boats and spend a lot of time down there at the harbour, but I prefer sailing to fishing.' Richard drew patterns on the cloth with a spoon, then looked up suddenly to meet her pensive eyes. 'Why the analytical look?'

'It just occurred to me that I'm dining with you—and enjoying it very much—yet I completely forgot to ask the question I should have asked before accepting your invitation.' Harriet pulled a face. 'What I'm trying to say is that a man your age is usually married, or something——'

'I am not,' he said at once, 'neither married nor anything else, at least not at this moment in time. So you need have no qualms on that score. I'm a lot older than you, I'm afraid, so unless you have a taste for maturity possibly you prefer your escorts younger.'

'No.' Harriet regarded him thoughtfully. 'I prefer my escorts unattached, rather than any particular age.'

'Then I qualify.' Richard leaned back in his chair and smiled. 'Tell me what you do with your life, Harriet.'

'Nothing very exciting,' she said, and told him about her job and flat, about her doctor brother and her father who taught languages in a large comprehensive school near Norwich. 'Terribly ordinary, really,' she finished.

'Men?' he asked.

She looked up sharply to surprise a fleeting look of cold analysis in his eyes, and a chill ran up her spine. His expression changed almost instantly to warmth, so quickly she was uncertain if it had been there at all, but the impression had been strong enough to alert her ingrained wariness towards the predatory male, for a few moments almost forgotten with this disturbingly attractive man.

'Yes,' she said, after a pause.

'Just "yes"?' Richard looked amused. 'Does that mean a lot of men, or one in particular?'

'Both.'

'Both?' He frowned.

'That's right. Lots of men friends and recently one in particular.' Harriet eyed him quizzically. 'Not, I'm certain, that it can be of any possible interest to you, but the latter is no longer friendly.'

'Ah! So that's why you're here—to mend a broken heart.'

'Nothing so romantic.' Harriet smiled coolly and gave him a flippant account of Harvey Jackson's surprise packet.

There was an odd, wry smile on Richard's face as he listened. 'And the rejected lover?' he asked.

'Jeremy was *not* my lover,' retorted Harriet. 'Not that it's really any of your business, but, just for the record, it was my refusal to grant him the privilege that actually caused the rift. He was hell-bent on moving in with me— he always did envy me my flat.'

Richard's crack of laughter turned heads at adjoining tables, but he seemed unaware of them, and leaned forward to take possession of Harriet's hands. She stared down at the slim brown fingers grasping hers, wanting to snatch her hands away, but too embarrassed to chance attracting further attention from the other diners.

'Surely it was your bed this chap was hell-bent on occupying, not your flat!' he said, and Harriet's head jerked up indignantly, unhappily aware of the unaccustomed tide of colour flooding her face for the second time that day, also that Richard was watching its progress in fascination. 'Does that happen regularly?' he asked.

'No, it does not,' said Harriet crossly, and tried to pull away, but the hard, calloused hands refused to loosen their grip.

'I had no intention of annoying you, Harriet,' he said, and looked at her in a way that quickened her pulse even more. 'But surely a girl as lovely as you must be used to male admiration?'

Harriet was. It was only Richard Livesey's in particular that was causing such havoc with her poise. She pulled herself together forcibly.

'I'd be a hypocrite if I denied it,' she said flatly. 'But I'm always pleased more by acknowledgement of my intellect than compliments about my looks.'

'A man has to be given the opportunity to explore the intellect beneath such an alluring exterior, Harriet—no, don't look so defensive. I promise to behave with perfect propriety.' His smile was reassuring. 'I'll take you back to the Miramar safe and sound, I swear.'

And true to his word he was on his feet at once, exchanging a few friendly words with the waiters as he paid the bill, and almost before she was ready Harriet was in the big white car and the evening was almost over. Richard drove back in silence, and she was conscious of a feeling of disappointment and anti-climax as the lights of the hotel came into view, then she stiffened as he drove past the lighted entrance and stopped the car in the dark, deserted car-park beyond.

'Don't be nervous, Harriet—I'm not about to demand instant compensation for the modest sum expended on your dinner.' There was palpable enjoyment in his deep voice and Harriet swung to face him, nettled.

'I didn't imagine you were.'

'Oh, yes, you did.' He leaned towards her. 'Instead of abduction, or even seduction, attractive prospect though it is—my object was to ask if I might see you again.'

Her eyes opened wide in an effort to see his expression, but in the darkness it was difficult to see whether he was laughing at her or not. One part of her was overjoyed that he wanted another meeting, but the sane, sensible side of her was vetoing such an unwise idea. As a holiday acquaintance Richard Livesey was too disturbing by half, and the best course would be to say thank you and good night and leave it at that.

He cut through her indecision, asking her if she'd been up to Monchique.

'I haven't been anywhere yet. I'm booked on a trip to Lisbon the day after tomorrow, but I'd thought to leave Monchique for next week.'

'Let me drive you there tomorrow. I promise to be an efficient guide.' His voice held a persuasive note it was hard to resist.

'I don't know——' she began uncertainly, but he seized on her uncertainty.

'Let me make up your mind. Have a rest by the pool after breakfast, then I'll call for you at, say, eleven-thirty. I guarantee a nice, leisurely trip, and have you back at the hotel in plenty of time for dinner.'

There seemed no point in hesitating. Offered the opportunity to pass the time in highly interesting company *and* see something of the Algarve only an idiot would refuse.

'All right, thank you.' She smiled at him in the darkness. 'I'd like that very much.'

'Good.' Richard helped her out of the car and walked the few yards to the hotel entrance with her, a hand under her elbow as he looked down at her in the bright lights under the hotel portico.

'Good night, Harriet. I'll look forward to tomorrow.'

Harriet smiled. 'So shall I, and thank you for the evening, and for the memorable dinner.'

He took her hand and held it lightly for a moment. 'The pleasure was all mine, Miss Harriet Neil.' He raised her hand to his lips and kissed it, which resulted in a decidedly breathless quality to her good night as she hurried through the revolving door into the hotel.

She could hear music coming from both lounge and bar, but went straight to the lift, reluctant to encounter the Armstrongs at the moment, nice people though they were. She was in no mood for questions and teasing. She wanted to lie in bed and think about the evening, go over it from start to finish while it was vivid in her mind, to review it rationally now that she was away from Richard Livesey's disturbing presence. She found she was staring into the mirror with wide, dreaming eyes, and came back to earth with a jolt. This was silly. She turned away sharply and began to undress, addressing herself succinctly on the folly of falling prey to the charms of tall dark strangers, particularly when the stranger in question had made her feel distinctly uneasy once or twice during the evening. She was fairly sure he was strongly attracted to her, or to her looks, more likely. But at the same time there was some indefinable something in his manner that made her brain hesitate even while her less cerebral side responded to him in a way no man had ever made it respond before. Harriet was justifiably proud of her common sense as a rule, but unfortunately it deserted her completely when she looked into the dark-blue eyes of Richard Livesey.

She groaned, and attacked her hair fiercely with a brush. It was quite simple, she told herself firmly. It was all right to go out with the man, and to enjoy his company, but losing her wits over him was definitely against the rules. What made it all so tricky was that she had never come up against a man who affected her like this before. Of course it was quite possible that Richard's brand of attraction owed a lot to circumstance and romantic surroundings. On a wet Monday morning in Leamington Spa he might seem just like any other man, Harriet argued, but failed to convince herself and climbed into bed with a sigh, to lie staring out at the moonlight.

She found it hard to believe that Richard had no motive in making her acquaintance beyond the usual one of a man drawn to her looks, that her physical charms were responsible for his interest. Which was stupid. What else could he be interested in? What was any man *ever* interested in, if it came to that? In the long run they were all more interested in the cover than the book, and no doubt Richard Livesey was no exception. Harriet gave herself a mental shake and put a halt to the introspection, told herself to stop being such a goose and just enjoy the outing with Richard next day in its proper perspective as a little diversion to liven her holiday.

The Armstrongs were spending the day in Albufeira, and they had left the dining-room next morning by the time Harriet arrived, breathless, only minutes before breakfast was officially over. After tossing and turning for most of the night she had overslept, and was only just in time to order coffee and toast. She hurried over it, then went to buy an English newspaper to read on her sunbed near the pool, and she settled down with it in the sunshine, eventually falling into a light doze. She woke with a start and found it was later than she thought, and dashed into the hotel to have a shower. Maddeningly there was suntan cream in her hair, which meant a shampoo and extra time to dry her damp mane, and by the time it was only partly dry Harriet found she was quite definitely late. She abandoned the damp mass and tied it at the nape of her neck with a black ribbon, then tugged on pink cotton dungarees over a strawberry-pink T-shirt, and hurled a few necessities into her big white bag before sprinting from her room to the lift, which, of course, was at ground-floor level and stopped at every floor on its way up to collect her from the fifth. She managed to run a bright pink lipstick over her lips as the lift took her down to the foyer, and she emerged with reasonable composure, considering the first person she laid eyes on was Richard, propped against the reception desk chatting to the girls behind it. His clothes were as offhand as hers; espadrilles, white cotton levis and a thin, dark-blue shirt, but in some indefinable way the effect was style—and money. Possibly it was the wafer-thin gold watch on his wrist, or the gold-rimmed sunglasses dangling from one long finger as he talked—whatever it was reminded Harriet that he'd never mentioned what he did for a living.

She strolled across the floor towards Richard and one of the receptionists caught sight of her and said something to him. He spun round and turned on the full power of his smile in greeting, and with a swift word of farewell over his shoulder to the girls he came swiftly towards her.

'Good morning. Do I find you well this morning?'

'Just fine—only a little late, I'm afraid.'

'Are you?' Richard glanced at the Rolex Oyster on his

wrist. 'I hadn't noticed.'

Harriet wished she'd taken the time to dry her hair properly since he was so unconcerned about her lateness, and preceded him from the hotel feeling distinctly nettled.

'You look delectable this morning, Harriet, though very young in that get-up.' He gave her a smiling glance as they drove off. 'I feel like an uncle taking a young niece out for a treat.'

She shot him a sardonic look. 'You don't strike me as the avuncular type, Richard.'

He put his sunglasses on and grinned, his teeth showing white in his dark face. 'Why not?'

'Maybe because my own uncles incline to thinning hair and thickening waistlines, darlings though they are!' They laughed together and Harriet gave a little involuntary sigh of pleasure as she relaxed against the leather upholstery and watched the scenery as they passed. 'I had a sort of virus a short time ago, and you know today, for the first time, I feel really back to normal again. A few more days of lotus-eating and I'll be better than before. Which is just as well,' she added. 'I'm not noble enough to suffer in silence.'

'Have you ever suffered very much at all?' he asked abruptly.

Harriet gave him a startled look. 'As much as any normal person of my age and background, I suppose,' she said quietly. 'Only a fool expects to go through life without reversal of some kind. Besides, tragedy is relative, or don't you think so?'

'*I* think we're becoming very introspective for such a beautiful day.' Richard's tone was light again. 'Let me play guide, as I promised. We are, at the moment, on the highway that runs across the Algarve, all the way from Vila Real do Santo Antonio, on the Spanish border, to Sagres in the west. Shortly we'll turn off on a minor road which will take us to an inn where we can enjoy a *churrasco* while gazing out over a view of orange groves.'

'Sounds promising. What's a *churrasco*?' Harriet was as ready to banish the sombre little moment as Richard.

'Barbecue. I think you'll like it.'

He was right. Harriet thoroughly enjoyed the fairly leisurely ride along the highway, glad Richard was not the type of driver compelled to hurtle along at a speed which made it impossible to take in the charm of the countryside. She was enchanted by it all, and exclaimed over every one of the famous chimneypots on the Algarvean houses they passed. The intricate filigree designs were a left-over from the Moors, Richard told her, evidence of whom was never very far away. Eventually they turned off on a country road that wound through plantations of bamboo and gnarled fig trees until they arrived at a *pousada* with red-tiled roof and whitewashed walls in brilliant relief against a backdrop of orange trees which marched in regimented lines as far as the eye could see.

'Idyllic!' breathed Harriet, enchanted by her surroundings.

Richard watched with indulgence in his eyes as she tucked into sizzling portions of barbecued chicken with unconcealed enthusiasm. The innkeeper served her himself, keeping her pottery goblet filled with sparkling *vinho verde* and smiling broadly at the rapture on her glowing face as she tasted the subtle flavour of garlic and spices on the meat. Only when mine host had satisfied himself that the beautiful *senhora* could eat no more did he retire and leave Richard and Harriet alone.

'At the risk of repeating myself I do like to see a woman enjoy her food,' commented Richard with a grin. 'Do you always eat with such single-minded enthusiasm?'

'No, indeed.' Harriet made a face and drank some wine. 'Sometimes—mainly when I work late—my attitude towards cooking gets a bit jaded.'

'Don't you ever get tired of living alone?' he asked, and she gave the question consideration for a moment or two.

'No, never. I like it. And if I do get a bit bored with my own company I can always run home to my parents for the weekend, or drive over to my brother's house. And during the week I go out quite a bit in the evenings.' She stretched luxuriously and undid the ribbon securing her hair, running her fingers through the still-damp strands. 'You don't mind, I hope. My hair refused to dry in time before I came out.'

Richard's eyes were inscrutable as they looked at the bright, rippling hair. '*I* don't mind. But I think the waiters, not to mention the *patrao*, might drop a few dishes any minute—they can't take their eyes off it.'

'It's because the colour's so gaudy,' she said with a sigh.

'Is it natural?'

Harriet shook her head sorrowfully. '*Et tu, Brute*? Yes, it is natural, and no, it isn't a perm, and now let's talk about something else more interesting.' She tied the offending hair back with a tight jerk of the ribbon. 'I do thank you for bringing me here,' she went on with resolute politeness. 'Portugal is such a beautiful country.'

The corners of Richard's mouth twitched, but he took his cue obediently. 'The Algarve isn't really typical of the rest of the country. It's quite a separate place, different in climate, and even now a strong influence still lingers from the Moors. They called it "The Place Beyond".'

'Literally out of this world,' she said pensively, and shook her head as he pressed her to more wine, her eyes on the serried green ranks of bushy orange trees under the brilliant blue sky. They were near the end of their yield, but were still studded with the last golden globes of fruit glowing, lantern-like, among the glossy green leaves.

After a time Richard stood up. 'Up you get. Our next stop is Silves, where you can absorb a little culture before we head for the purely geographical delights of Monchique.'

They spent an hour in Silves, once the capital of the

Algarve, but the time was hardly long enough to appreciate the full charm of the town crouching sleepily in the afternoon sun below the domination of the great red castle. The castle, with the cathedral, was the only survivor of the great 1755 earthquake which also laid most of Lisbon flat, Richard told Harriet, and she shivered, picturing the devastation only too easily, suddenly glad to leave her contemplation of the cathedral's splendid rococo altar and walk in the sunshine again as they went back to the car.

'Are you tired?' asked Richard.

'No, of course not.' Harriet smiled at him serenely. 'Perhaps less of the *vinho verde* might have been more sensible, but otherwise I'm fine. Lead on, Macduff!'

'Obviously not a superstitious lady or you'd be wary of references to *Macbeth*.' Richard glanced at her quizzically as he started the car.

'Don't tell me you're a prey to superstition,' she said, surprised.

'I'm not. I believe we make our own luck, shape our own destinies.' Richard gave her a disarming smile, then kept his attention on the road. 'But let's not get introspective again, Harriet. Turn your eyes to the scenery and tell me if it pleases you.'

It could hardly fail, as Harriet assured him with sincerity. The road was climbing upwards through mountainsides where chestnut trees grew in profusion cheek by jowl with mimosa and another tree which Richard said she might know best as arbutus.

'But in Portugal they call it the *medronho*, and make the red berries into a fierce liqueur of the same name; a speciality of the Algarve.'

They passed through the village of Monchique itself, with its steep terraces of houses, and took the road that looped upwards above it, circling the mountain in dizzying curves that made Harriet cling to her seat during the five kilometres between the village and the mountain top. When they reached it there was a plateau

with space for cars to park and for several stalls laid out
with local pottery and knitted goods to tempt the tourist.
Harriet stood with Richard for some time, gazing down
in wonder at half of southern Portugal laid out in
spectacular panorama far below, before turning back
eagerly to browse through the goods on offer. She left the
bargaining to Richard's fluent Portuguese and quickly
acquired a heavy white Aran-type sweater for what
seemed an amazingly low price.

'Are you sure that's enough money, Richard?' Harriet
was doubtful as she handed over the notes to the smiling
woman behind the stall. 'It seems very cheap to me—I
wish I'd cashed a few more travellers' cheques before I
came out. I could have bought more.'

Richard reached for his wallet. 'Let me pay for
whatever you want and——'

'No, really!' She could have kicked herself. 'I didn't
mean——'

'I know you didn't.' He smiled down at her, his thick
hair lifting in the stiffish breeze. 'You could always pay
me back when we reach the Miramar.'

She looked away, embarassed, and shook her head.
'Yes, of course, but I won't, thank you. I'm sure I'll see
plenty of other things before I go back. In fact,' she
added, as they went back to the car, 'I saw the most
wonderful ceramic in a tiny little shop in Praia do Ceu—
fruit and vegetables in a great tumble of colour, all done
by the young girl there on the premises. I could just
picture it on the wall in my flat, but it was too big to
juggle with on the flight home.' Harriet was conscious
she was babbling in her efforts to cover the awkward
moment, and busied herself with the seatbelt as they got
in the car.

Richard turned in his seat, bending his head slightly to
look into her face. 'You're embarrassed,' he said bluntly.
'Are you afraid I'll think you were mercenary?'

'The thought did cross my mind. I like to pay my own
way.'

'I meant the money only as a temporary loan.'

'Yes, I know. Thank you.' She smiled at him briefly. 'But I wouldn't have been able to pay you back today. The bureau de change, or whatever it's called here, will be closed by the time we get back, and that would mean——' She stopped, her cheeks growing warm.

'And that would mean meeting me again.' Richard lightly touched her hand with long, brown fingers. 'And you wouldn't like that?'

She turned away, afraid he would see her reaction to his touch. 'I hadn't thought about it.'

'Then think about it now. Will you dine with me tomorrow night?'

There was persistence, rather than urgency, in his voice and she turned wide thoughtful eyes on his face. 'Why?'

He smiled with irritating indulgence. 'I would have thought that was obvious—because I enjoy your company.'

Harriet frowned. 'It all seems so—so contrived, somehow.'

'Contrived?' he said sharply.

'Well, stereotyped, then. Girl on holiday alone in Portugal, handsome stranger tailor-made to inject a little colour into her holiday.' She shrugged. 'I find the situation a bit suspect, that's all.'

'You're over-cautious—still smarting over your recent romantic setback.' Richard leaned back in his seat with his arms folded, his long legs stretched out in front of him as far as the car interior would allow. 'What possible reason could I have for wanting to see you other than the obvious one of a man wanting the company of a beautiful woman?'

Put that way it made Harriet feel rather foolish. 'I'm sorry. Put it down to wariness because I'm playing away, I suppose.'

'Ah—a football fan?'

'No fear!' Suddenly Harriet chuckled, giving him a

sparkling look. 'If anything perhaps the sport ought to be show-jumping.'

Richard looked baffled. 'Show-jumping?'

She giggled. 'When you asked me to dinner the first time I didn't say yes, after all—I suppose I was awarding myself three points for a refusal!'

He laughed with her and took the wind completely out of her sails by bending to plant a hard, swift kiss on her smiling mouth. 'The correct term is three *faults*,' he said, grinning as he turned the car to begin the descent. 'You see! Subconsciously you must have wanted to accept right away. Where shall we go tomorrow?' he went on in exactly the same tone of voice, as though she had never voiced any doubts at all.

One way and another Harriet was completely routed, even though she made one more feeble attempt at protest. 'If I say I won't come does that mean I can expect you underfoot at the hotel tomorrow?'

'Of course!' he retorted. 'Where else? I'm at your feet already.'

Harriet gave up. 'Oh, very well. But fairly late, please. I want to spend a lazy day at the pool tomorrow, trying to augment my tan. I must be up at the crack of dawn the day after to go to Lisbon so I'll need to marshal my forces. I gather it's a fairly gruelling trip.'

'Whatever you say. I'll take you out for a quiet dinner and have you back as early as you like to go to bed. That suit you?'

It suited her admirably, but Harriet had no intention of telling Richard Livesey just how much on such short acquaintance, so she merely thanked him prettily and settled down to enjoy the journey back to Praia do Ceu.

Dinner alone in the restaurant later that evening seemed more than a little flat, loth though she was to admit it. The food was excellent, and by now several friendly smiles were directed at her as she made her way to her table. But without conversation as a sauce—and Richard Livesey's conversation in particular—the meal definitely lacked something. The Armstrongs were at their table and gathered Harriet up in their train as they left in search of coffee after the meal, and a pleasant hour went by in the bar exchanging notes on their various activities during the day, Harriet's excursion, not to mention her escort, attracting much interest from all sides.

'Made a hit there by the look of it, my girl!' George Armstrong's genial opinion was shared by all his family, and Harriet laughed, too wise to make protestations no one was likely to believe, particularly when she was obliged to admit that Richard Livesey was taking her out yet again the following evening.

'Take care, won't you, dear,' said Dora anxiously.

'Harriet's only having a meal with him, Mother,' teased Tony. 'Livesey doesn't look like a white-slave-trafficker, or anything like that.'

'I don't suppose there's anything like that,' murmured Jane, grinning from ear to ear.

'Well, you never know—look at Crippen,' said Dora. Her husband looked at her blankly. 'What's Crippen go to do with it?'

'*He* didn't look like a murderer, George. People don't wear labels, you know.'

George Armstrong didn't join in the young people's amusement. 'She's got a point. What does this fellow do for a living, Harriet?'

She smiled apologetically. 'I've no idea, Mr Armstrong. I haven't asked him. I could always have a word with the hotel owner, though, he knows Richard well, apparently.'

This reassured Mrs Armstrong somewhat, not that Harriet had any actual intention of checking up on Richard. It was pointless in the light of how short a time she would know him. Besides, she reflected ruefully, she was looking forward to dinner with him and didn't want to learn anything about him that might make it necessary to cancel it. He had been quite definite about his bachelor status, and that was the only thing of any concern to her, so anything else was best left undiscovered.

The Armstrong men were forgoing their golf next day to take their ladies up to Monchique, and Harriet's glowing account of her day whetted their appetites, particularly when the ladies heard about the sweater.

'Take plenty of money,' Harriet advised as she said good night, and giggled at the concerted groan she got from the two men in response.

Lying by the pool next day she admitted to herself that her idle day in the sun was made doubly pleasant by the prospect of dinner with Richard in the evening afterwards. Perhaps tonight would be the last time she would see him. By the time she came back to Praia do Ceu from Lisbon he might have left for whatever place he called home, which could be the Hindu Kush for all she knew. Harriet turned on her stomach to watch the bathers in the pool, restless at the thought of never seeing Richard Livesey again. She was sorry now she had booked on the Lisbon trip, but decided against cancelling it on the mere off chance Richard would be on hand to amuse her if she stayed behind.

After lunch in the Miramar dining-room for a change Harriet decided to take a walk down to the village once the midday period of rest was over. She was bored with her inactivity and needed exercise, despite the heat, and walked down to the shops to look at the ceramic and exchange a few words with the pretty young girl who had created it. She hadn't intended to buy anything but consoled herself with a plate painted with Portugal's symbolic cockerel. It would give her good luck, the young artist assured her, and Harriet took it back to the hotel wondering how she could interpret the term 'luck'. She hoped it meant not having to say goodbye to Richard for good tonight, then laughed at herself and spent the rest of the afternoon on the terrace reading and trying not to think too much of the evening ahead.

Richard was waiting for her in the foyer when she went down promptly at eight. His face lit up with the now familiar smile when he caught sight of her, and Harriet breathed in deeply to steady herself. He was wearing the formal grey suit of their first encounter in the hotel and she was pleased she had taken extra pains with her appearance, opting for simplicity in a suit of almond-green rough-textured linen. The severity of the long straight skirt and collarless thigh-length jacket was softened by the raw silk of the camisole blouse in the same colour, and she had chosen her highest-heeled shoes to wear with it, linen in a shade or two darker than the suit. Even her hair had been severely disciplined into its plaited coil in keeping with the rest of her.

'Good evening, Harriet.' Richard took her hand and gave her a comprehensive look from head to toe. 'A vision of quite formidable elegance tonight, if I'm permitted to say so.'

'You are.' She smiled at him brilliantly, every nerve-end tingling at the sight of this big, dark man and the touch of his hand on hers as they left the hotel.

'Have you enjoyed your day?' he asked as he drove off.

'I've had a very nice day indeed; sinfully lazy, but lovely. And you?'

'Rather busy. I leave for the north tomorrow.' Richard's attention was on the road and he missed the look of blank dismay Harriet knew only too well was on her face North? Where? Africa, America—the North Pole, even. He was hardly the most communicative man she'd ever met, that was certain.

'And I'm off to Lisbon,' she said lightly, 'so we scatter in all directions. Where are we going tonight, by the way?' she added, noticing they were travelling in the opposite direction from the last time.

'Not far. To Porches, a village a few kilometres down the road. There's a rather interesting restaurant there called *O Leao de Porches*, The Lion of Porches. They serve excellent food, and I rather fancy you'll like the building. It's a fine example of a seventeenth-century farmhouse, and very sympathetically converted to its present use.'

'Sounds delightful.' Harriet hesitated, then plunged into the subject that had been bothering her to quite an extent while she was getting ready for the evening. 'Actually, Richard, I was wondering how I can repay your hospitality. Would you allow me to pay for the meal tonight? I mean, you've already——'

The look he turned on her silenced her very effectively, making her quail. 'The next time a woman pays for my dinner will be the first,' he said succinctly. 'If I invite a lady to dine I foot the bill—without exception.'

'All right, all right,' she said hurriedly. 'It's just that I felt guilty about accepting so much hospitality——'

'Forget it.'

One look at Richard's profile was enough to make her change the subject swiftly, and she chatted away at speed about her walk down to the village to see her beloved ceramic.

'I lust after it,' she said cheerfully, 'but had to content myself with a very superior version of the national cockerel for my flat instead. Guaranteed to bring me good luck, I was told.'

'Do you need good luck?' he asked casually.

'Doesn't everyone?'

'If you're so set on this ceramic why don't you ask the girl to do a smaller version for you?'

'I never thought of that!' Harriet was much struck by the idea, and gave him a mischievous smile. 'Too bad you have to leave tomorrow—you could have acted as interpreter for me.'

There was no answering smile from him. 'The trip is very necessary, unfortunately.' He gave her a very deliberate sidelong look. 'If it weren't, Harriet, believe me I'd call it off.'

Harriet sat digesting this in silence until they arrived at the restaurant which, as Richard had promised, was very pleasing to the eye. It stood near the church in the centre of Porches, and opened off a whitewashed courtyard, filled with tubs of the inevitable geraniums. Inside, a small bar led into a large room with a vaulted, raftered ceiling and a big stone fireplace with a fire burning in it, to Harriet's surprise.

'The walls are so thick it could be quite chilly in here at this time of day otherwise,' explained Richard when they were settled at their table.

'It's quite lovely.' Harriet pointed to the row of exquisite plates on a ledge running high round the walls, handpainted in various colours and designs. 'And talking of pottery!'

'Those are the work of an Englishman, Patrick Swift, who founded the Olaria pottery a short distance from here.' Richard smiled at her openly displayed enthusiasm for her surroundings and helped her choose the meal, which was deceptively simple. They ate perfectly grilled sole followed by a dish of piquantly flavoured liver cooked in thin strips, and were served by young waiters in black trousers and white shirts with red sashes round their waists. Harriet enjoyed watching them move among the diners, their very appearance adding to her pleasure. I shall remember this, she thought. Afterwards.

Richard kept her glass filled with the full-bodied red Dao wine he liked best, though he drank sparingly himself, mindful, she supposed, of the drive back.

'You look a little daunting tonight, Harriet,' he said after coffee had been served.

'Daunting?' Her dark eyes widened with surprise.

'Tonight you're the archetypal modern woman, self-supporting and independent—not much like the wild-haired creature in dungarees of yesterday.' He lit a cigar after asking her permission, and let the smoke rise between them in an aromatic screen.

'Just one of the many facets of my personality.' Harriet intended the words as a joke, and felt rather chilled at the rather calculating look in Richard's narrowed eyes.

'And would I like the other facets?' His words held a definite challenge that unsettled her, but before she could question it he changed the subject and pressed her to try some *medronho*, the liqueur made from the berries of the arbutus trees she had seen the day before.

Her eyes glinted. 'It will be your fault if I sing vulgar songs on the way back!'

Richard laughed and signalled to a waiter, and shortly afterwards fresh coffee appeared in front of them accompanied by two narrow, tube-shaped liqueur glasses filled with colourless liquid.

'Drink it like this,' instructed Richard, and tossed down the spirit in one swallow, following it immediately with a mouthful of coffee. Harriet followed suit obediently, then gasped as a tremendous heat flashed through her body. Her eyes opened wide in consternation, filling with involuntary tears for an instant.

'You could have warned me!' she gasped. 'I think I'll take off my jacket.'

Richard rose to help her and she felt better at once in her brief camisole top. The narrow straps revealed her shoulders in all the glory of their pale gilding of suntan, and Richard's eyes rested on them in frank admiration.

'Much, much better,' he commented as he sat down again. 'With the jacket on you look elegant, but remote and cool. Like that, with those beautiful bare shoulders, you look all woman, and infinitely more approachable.'

Harriet's eyebrows rose. 'I'm not sure I care for that, somehow.'

He smiled quizzically. 'You must surely know the effect on a mere male of a brief little garment like that.'

'I dress to please myself,' she said with emphasis.

'You believe that?' His smile plainly proclaimed he did not.

'Certainly.' Harriet's pleasure in the evening diminished and she slid her arms back into the jacket and picked up her bag. She directed a cool little smile at Richard's watchful face and rose to her feet. 'You said you'd take me back whenever I was ready. I'm ready now.'

The look he gave her as he got up was thoughtful and rather disconcerting. 'You mean I've genuinely upset you by my remark?'

'Goodness, no,' she lied, and gave a brittle little laugh. 'But I have to be up early tomorrow, as I said before.'

Richard paid the bill and escorted her outside, placing an impersonal hand under her elbow as they crossed the cobbled courtyard to the car in silence. So this was it, thought Harriet bleakly; a drive back to the hotel, a polite thank you and good night, with not even a holiday snap as a memento of the tall dark stranger the tour company had not included as an extra.

'You're very quiet,' remarked Richard after they'd been driving for a while. 'You didn't enjoy the evening?'

'Yes, of course I did,' she said quietly. 'Both the restaurant and the meal were quite perfect.'

'Then it was my company that palled so quickly.'

'I didn't mean that.'

'But my remark needled you into leaving, just the same.' His voice sounded harsher than usual and Harriet shivered.

'You made me feel cheap, as though I'd dressed deliberately to tease,' she said honestly.

'I didn't mean to offend you, Harriet—I don't want to leave you with a sour taste in your mouth after the pleasant times we've spent together.'

Pleasant times, she thought dully. So that was how he would remember her—as a pleasant little interlude. If, of course, he ever thought of her at all once they had parted.

'It's not that late, Harriet. Surely you don't have to go back yet?' His voice had softened, an unaccustomed cajoling note in it that reacted on her strongly. 'Let me drive you a very short way off the beaten track. There's a headland a short distance along the cliff where I can park the car and we can watch the moon rising over the sea, and count the lights of the fishing boats, and we can talk

of shoes and ships and sealing-wax and I solemnly
promise not to make any further remarks calculated to
provoke you. Agreed?'

Relief flooded Harriet, and she gave her consent, as
she rather thought he'd known she would. It was what
she wanted very much anyway, if she were honest, to be
with him even a little while longer, and away from other
eyes for once. 'As long as we don't stay for more than a
few minutes,' she felt obliged to add. 'I meant it about not
being late.'

Only five minutes or so later Richard brought the car
to a halt on a small patch of open ground almost at the
edge of the cliff where they could look down on the sea, as
he had said. Away to the left the lights of Praia do Ceu
twinkled in the distance, giving Harriet an irrational
feeling of security as she gazed at the moon, which was
painting a silver path of light across the sea as it rose, a
sight so beautiful it brought a lump to her throat and
made her eyes wet. It brought emphasis where none was
needed to the poignancy of these last minutes shared
with the man beside her.

'It must be your evening for being quiet,' said Richard
softly.

She cleared her throat. 'You were the one who wanted
to talk.'

'Then I was lying.' He turned to her swiftly, his broad
shoulders outlined against the luminous sky. 'At the risk
of incurring your displeasure again I must be honest and
admit talk is not uppermost in my mind at this precise
moment.'

Harriet's mouth dried and she sat very still. Richard
muttered something deep in his throat and the next
moment pulled her into his arms and kissed her with a
hard demand she responded to involuntarily. She had no
thought of denying him. If any thought remained in her
mind at all it was the fleeting recognition that this was
what had been implicit between them from the very first,
from the moment when a look from a ragged fisherman

had made her heart somersault beneath her ribs. It was behaving erratically now, beating like a wild thing as his mouth moved in triumphant certainty on hers and his arms held her cruelly tight against his chest.

After a long, heart-bursting interval he firmly raised his head a little and stared down at her, breathing hard. 'Well?' he demanded roughly. 'Was I wrong? Wasn't this what you wanted as much as I did?'

'Yes,' she panted, and tried to pull away. 'Yes, it was. I admit it freely. But you must let me go now— please——'

'I don't think I can,' he muttered thickly, and bent his mouth to hers again.

Harriet did her best to struggle, but the arms that held her were like bands of steel, and she didn't really want him to let her go anyway. The merest touch of his lips on hers had melted what resistance she had against him, which wasn't much in the first place. Shivering and helpless she lay against him in a pliant response that sent tremors through Richard's hard body. His fingers were at her neck, undoing the knot in frantic haste and running through the gleaming strands that showed bright even in the moonlit darkness. He raised his head and gazed at the silken mass, then down at her face. Harriet stared back, mesmerised, then her lids dropped to hide from the naked desire on the handsome face that up to now had been so detached and controlled. Then Richard's wide, expressive mouth was on hers again and his need was something she shared. She could feel the tide of it rising within herself, rushing through her to make her breasts ache and her entire body yearn. He slid the jacket from her shoulders, holding her fast with one hand while the other moved over her throat with a delicacy that made her tremble. Then he raised his head and looked deep into her eyes as he removed his restraining arm, and her head fell back against the seat and her body leapt in response as very gently he slid the straps of her silk camisole down over her shoulders and bent his head until his mouth touched her breast.

For a moment she was conscious only of the weight of his head and the touch of his hair as it lay against her skin, then he moved and his mouth found a vulnerable nipple. His teeth captured and teased it, and a low, shuddering moan escaped from her as her head turned from side to side at the almost unbearable sensation. His long fingers caressed and teased each nipple in turn while his mouth laid siege to its twin, until her hands clutched convulsively at his dark hair and she pleaded with him in a voice she hardly recognised as her own.

Richard sat up and pulled her into his arms, holding her close again, tipping her head back with ungentle fingers. 'Please what, Harriet?' he said hoarsely. 'Please stop? Please go on? What shall I do? What shall *we* do? I want you—touch me. See how much I want you.' And he caught her hand and placed it where she could feel the hard throbbing of his need through his clothes.

It was the last straw. Harriet shook her head wildly and tore herself out of his arms, utterly overwhelmed by this sudden onslaught of feeling between them, suspicious of it and conscious now that this was all there was. Just tonight, then nothing; only regrets. With tremendous effort she drew up the straps of her blouse with shaking fingers, burningly aware of the tension she could feel in the powerful body so close to hers.

'I want you too, Richard,' she said breathlessly. 'It must be only too obvious how much. But I'm not going to let you make love to me—more than you have done already,' she added, aware that he had been making love to her with devastating effect for the past few minutes.

Richard wrenched himself away and sat back in his seat, his harsh breathing audible in the confines of the car. 'Why not?' he asked after a lengthy interval.

'I don't go in for one-night stands.' Harriet bent to find her discarded jacket and shrugged herself into it, pulling it together across her chest.

'Not much point in doing that,' he said with irony. 'I've seen those beautiful breasts and touched them, and

I'll be plagued by thoughts of them for the rest of the night—and for other nights to come, no doubt.'

'I think it's time we went.' She felt unequal to any more emotion. She dreaded saying goodbye, and at the same time longed for it with equal intensity.

'Come outside and stroll with me,' he said, surprising her, and slid out of his seat, coming round to help her out of the car. They walked in silence to the edge of the cliff, the cool breeze lifting Harriet's tumbled hair and cooling her hot cheeks. They stood without saying a word for some time, then very gently Richard reached for her hand, his eyes fixed on the sea below.

'I never meant that to happen, Harriet. Believe me, it was quite unpremeditated.' He ran his free hand through his hair and sighed. 'I won't say the thought of kissing you never crossed my mind. I'd be lying if I did. I've had thoughts of doing just that from the moment I first laid eyes on you, but I never imagined what would happen if I did.' He gave a short, mirthless laugh. 'No wonder that poor fool of a boy-friend of yours wanted to move in with you!'

Harriet felt too drained to take offence. 'That was different,' she said dully.

'I don't want to hear about it.' Richard kicked at some loose pebbles with the toe of one elegant black leather shoe. 'It's my own reaction I'm concerned about.'

'Isn't everyone!'

'I meant that I never intended to fall on you like an animal—not my usual style at all, in fact.' Richard's voice was heavy with self-disgust.

Harriet contemplated telling him that her own reactions had hardly been typical of her own behaviour, either, but she couldn't summon up the energy. She sighed and turned away towards the car. He followed her, and stood leaning against the bonnet, smoking a cigar while she combed her hair and reknotted it, her hands unsteady under the scrutiny of the blue eyes watching her.

'You could put on the light,' he said, but she shook her head, afraid her face might reveal too much.

'I shall miss you,' said Richard abruptly.

'I'll miss you too,' returned Harriet.

'I wish we could have had more time together.'

'So do I.'

'We *could* spend a little more time together if you wished,' he said, and ground out the stub of his cigar.

She eyed him warily as he got in the car. 'How?'

'I'm driving north tomorrow, and I take it you still mean to go to Lisbon.'

'Yes.'

'Come with me.'

Harriet frowned. 'Where?'

'Just as far as Lisbon—it's only a short distance out of my way.'

'But I'm booked on the coach.'

'So what? We could drive together, dine together, after which I deliver you to the hotel where the rest of the party is staying, and then you can return here next day on the coach.' Richard put a hand over hers and gripped it hard. 'It would mean another day together and I swear not to lay a finger on you again.'

'But the coach——'

He lifted her hand and kissed it. 'Tell them in the morning. Or I can tell Manoel Pires the courier myself when I come for you. What time are you due to leave?'

'Seven.' Harriet looked at him doubtfully. 'But Richard, I can't, it isn't practical——'

'I refuse to believe that you're unfailingly practical at all times, Harriet Neil.' He smiled at her, undermining her resolve very successfully.

'The people on the coach will think we occupied our time with less edifying pastimes than sightseeing,' she said bluntly.

'Let them think what they like,' he said indifferently. 'All I want is a little extra time with you—daytime, not night. Then I'll leave you at the hotel in Lisbon and

continue to the north and you can return to Praia do Ceu
to enjoy the rest of your holiday. The trip would be a lot
more pleasant in my car than in a coach, you know.'

'I'm sure it would, but that's hardly the point!'

'What *is* the point?'

Harriet looked at him searchingly, trying to see his
expression in the moonlight. 'Is this enthusiasm for my
company influenced by the rather stormy passage just
now, or had you thought of it while our relationship was
still entirely impersonal?'

'Speaking for myself I've never felt entirely impersonal as far as you're concerned,' he said mockingly. 'But
I assure you that the idea of travelling together was my
reason for bringing you out here to talk in the first place.
What happened next was one of those unforeseen
circumstances beyond my control. My intention was one
kiss—honour bright!'

Harriet laughed unwillingly. 'I'd like to travel with
you, but my common sense thinks it's a rotten idea.'

'Life would be very dull if we let common sense rule us
all the time.' Richard leaned towards her to look deep
into her eyes. 'You're on holiday, Harriet, relax a little—
come with me in the car; please.'

She returned the look steadily for a moment, then
nodded. 'All right. But I have conditions.'

He sighed and sat back in his seat. 'I can make a rough
guess at one of them, at least. Hands off, I suppose.'

'Exactly!'

'Any others?'

'Just one. I'd like you to tell me what you do for a
living.'

Richard laughed out loud, and squeezed her hand
hard. 'With pleasure, Harriet. I'm a farmer.'

CHAPTER THREE

HARRIET woke to a tap on her door the following morning, and fell out of bed feeling as though she'd only just fallen into it. Wrapped in her dressing-gown she took the tray from the waiter and subsided on the bed to drink her coffee and chew sleepily on a slice of toast. Amazing to have slept so soundly, she thought, yawning. After Richard's lovemaking she had expected to toss and turn all night, but from the look of the bed she could hardly have moved a muscle. And to think he was a farmer! The last profession she would have guessed at—banker, or stockbroker perhaps, but never anything to do with farming. Arable farming, he had told her, and the farm had been inherited from his parents, who were both dead, and at that point she was back at the hotel and it was time to say good night. There'd been no kiss as Richard left her to the early night she'd stipulated, and Harriet had fallen into bed feeling more worn out by the events of the evening than by a hard day's work.

It took only a few moments to shower and wake herself properly, and after packing an overnight bag she put on a cornflower-blue linen skirt, a white shirt and a chunky white sweater, and decided on flat white sandals as best for sightseeing, scooped up her hair into a loose knot on top of her head and went down to meet Richard. He was before her, deep in conversation with Manoel, the courier, and Harriet could see the coach outside the hotel, already full of passengers waiting to be off. Both men turned as she arrived, and the young Portuguese smiled at her cheerfully.

'*Bom dia*, Miss Neil. A change of plan, I hear.'

'Good morning. Yes—I hope it's not inconveniencing you in any way.' Harriet felt a little flustered when

Richard moved to her side and took her arm in a manner that brought a smile to Manoel's face again.

'No, no,' he assured her. 'Have a nice trip.'

'*Obrigad*', Manoel,' said Richard. '*Boa viagem.*'

'*É você tambem. Ate logo.*' The young man ran off to board the coach and Richard grinned down at Harriet's embarrassed face.

'Bothered by the publicity?'

She pulled a face. 'A bit.'

He chuckled and picked up her bag. 'Come on, let's get moving. We've a few kilometres to put on the clock today.' He waved goodbye to the sleepy-eyed receptionist just coming on duty, and with an arm round Harriet's waist hurried her outside to the waiting Mercedes.

He took off his grey suede windbreaker and slung it on the back seat with Harriet's bag, then leaned across and dealt with the seatbelt she had forgotten to fasten, smiling at her, his face dark in the early light above his open white collar and Cambridge-blue sweater.

'Ready?' he asked and touched her cheek lightly with one finger.

At his touch Harriet's doubts vanished and her heart suddenly felt as light as a balloon. She smiled and nodded, settling back in her seat to make the most of these last few hours with Richard. As they drove he told her about other places she should visit in the Algarve, and advised her to come again in February, when the almond trees were in bloom.

'I don't suppose there'll be a next time,' said Harriet.

'Why not? Don't you like it here?'

'Of course I do! From what I've seen of it so far it's the most beautiful place for a holiday one could wish for.' Harriet gave a little laugh. 'But I'm a working girl, Richard. I can't afford exotic holidays at the drop of a hat—I'm only here this time courtesy of Mr Jackson's mother-in-law.'

'Is your salary inadequate, then?'

'No, indeed. It's quite good for the area where I live,

but as I said before, I choose to live in my rather expensive flat alone rather than share the expenses with someone. Also I run a car. It's old and battered, but at least I can take off to see my parents or my brother whenever I want—represents freedom, I suppose. I value my independence. It's all a question of priorities, really—if I shared a flat with four other girls and cycled to work I could go abroad every year, no doubt, but I happen to prefer it my way.'

There was an odd, set look to Richard's face as he concentrated on the road. 'And has no one ever tried to make you give up this valued independence of yours?'

'Yes. I told you—my accountant friend Jeremy quite recently.'

'I meant marriage, Harriet.'

She shot a surprised look at him. 'No. Besides, marriage is a big step, and I'd rather not take it for years yet. I don't intend to marry until I'm perfectly sure I'm ready to commit myself to a permanent relationship. I'd want marriage to be for life.'

'And until you find the ideal partner I assume you intend to enjoy life to the full—make the most of what it offers.' Richard slanted a wry smile at her. 'What a sensible lady you are, Harriet.'

'Not really,' she said quietly, 'or I wouldn't be sitting here with you now. I'd be on the coach with the others.'

'So there must be some romance in that practical head.' He laughed. 'No one looking at that hair and face would credit the prosaic workings of the mind behind them. Didn't you ever consider going in for modelling, or something in the theatrical line?'

'No,' she said flatly, and scowled.

'Ah!' He flicked an amused glance at her face. 'Methinks I probe a nerve. The lady has been asked all that before.'

'She has indeed, *ad nauseam*, so let's talk of something else.'

'Then I'll return to my recommendation of almond-blossom time in the Algarve.'

'I'll keep it in mind.'

'There's a very romantic legend connected with it. It's said in these parts that a Moorish chief married a princess from the far north and brought her here to live, but she pined, homesick for the snows of her homeland. So her Moor planted his entire domain with almond trees, and hey presto, in spring the land was covered with snow-white blossom as far as the eye could see as a token of his true love.' The deep voice held a soft, teasing note that sent a tiny *frisson* of reaction along Harriet's spine.

'I trust the lady was suitably appreciative afterwards,' she said, deliberately flippant.

'Oh, I imagine so—happy-ever-after material, surely!'

After that the conversation centred mainly on less emotive subjects, even though Harriet found herself parting with a great deal of information about herself without learning very much more about her companion. She found it difficult to pose direct questions to him and let him take the lead in the conversation, which covered everything from the colour of her politics to her taste in music.

They stopped once briefly for coffee, but Richard was soon at the wheel again. 'I'd like to press on to Alcacer do Sal before we stop for lunch,' he said. 'All right with you?'

'Fine.' Harriet was more than content to stay beside him indefinitely as they drove through the sunbaked plains of the Alentejo.

'They call this region the storehouse of Portugal. Did you know two-thirds of the world's output of cork comes from the Alentejo?'

Harriet was bound to confess she did not. 'I've never even heard of the place before,' she said honestly. 'Geography was not my strong subject in school.'

'What *did* you like?'

'Maths, Chemistry—and English, oddly enough,

which is why I ended up doing business studies, I suppose.'

'You're a surprising creature, Harriet.'

She kept her eyes on the road, which was lined with fluttering-leaved eucalyptus trees, and cut directly through the glowing gold of wheatfields in the midday sun.

'I'm very ordinary, Richard; no surprises, really. Which is more than can be said for you. The last thing I would have thought of as far as you're concerned is farming.'

'Why? Surely my face is weatherbeaten enough, and these lines at the corners of my eyes are the penalty for long hours spent squinting into the sun,' he said, grinning at her.

'You're very lucky to get enough sun to make you squint,' she retorted, but at that moment he pointed out a row of girls working in the wheatfield with skirts tucked up above heavy boots, and the subject was forgotten.

Harriet was hot and thirsty by the time they were eventually seated at a table in one of the numerous cafés overlooking the river in Alcacer do Sal.

'Hungry?' asked Richard.

'Very! What do you recommend?'

'Are you game to try one of the regional dishes?'

'Of course.'

'Then how about some true Alentejo soup—*acorda Alentejana*?'

Harriet nodded eagerly, and Richard ordered their meal, then leaned his elbows on the table and looked into her eyes with a sudden intimacy that made her catch her breath.

'Don't look at me like that, Richard,' she said in a stifled voice, as all pretence of impersonal friendliness vanished abruptly, like raindrops in the sand.

'I can't help remembering last night,' he said softly.

She stared back at him helplessly. 'Neither can I.' She tore her eyes away from his and drank some of the sparkling *agua mineral* in her glass. 'But there's no point in it. I made conditions, remember.'

'I know. I'm sorry——' Richard broke off as the waiter arrived with two steaming soup bowls, then laughed at the look on Harriet's face as one of them was set in front of her.

'There's a poached egg in it!' she exclaimed. 'What else? Do you know?'

'Oh, at a rough guess, chopped bacon, smoked ham, onions, garlic and so on. Do you like it?' he added as she tasted it.

She nodded, mouth full. 'Heavenly—I was starving.'

To Richard's amusement she despatched the bowlful of steaming soup quickly, then tried the *queijinho fresco*, the cottage cheese provided for nibbling between courses.

'You obviously enjoyed that,' observed Richard drily. 'What would you like for a main course?'

She gazed at him in consternation. 'I thought that *was* my main course!'

'Not a bit of it. *Acorda Alentejana* is only for openers. Now you must have something else—it could be quite some time before your next meal.'

After much poring over the menu Harriet was persuaded to try some seafood rissoles after which, delicious though they were, she felt she never wanted to eat again, and refused even coffee to follow.

'You'll be thirsty,' warned Richard as they set off again.

'I know,' she wailed, 'but I'm so full I just don't have room!'

Just as Richard had predicted, she was very thirsty indeed after only a very short distance in the brilliant afternoon sunshine, and though she tried to hide it as best she could he soon turned off on a side road and stopped the car in the shade of some eucalyptus trees. He got out and opened the boot of the car, returning with an insulated flask in his hand. He unscrewed the top, filled it with fruit juice and handed it to her.

'I brought it in case of emergency,' he said. 'Drink it slowly.'

The ice-cold juice was delicious and not too sweet, almost bitter, but very refreshing to Harriet's grateful palate. It was an effort not to gulp it down greedily as she drank the whole beakerful under Richard's watchful gaze.

'That was marvellous,' she sighed. 'What is it?'

'*Suco de maracuja*—juice of the passionfruit,' he said, with a slight twist to his mobile mouth.

She eyed the flask in his hand. 'Aren't you having any?'

He shook his head. 'I drank beer and mineral water with my lunch. I'm not thirsty.'

'Do you think I could have a little more, then, please?'

Richard half-filled the beaker and sat watching as she drained it with only slightly less avidity than the first one. Harriet smiled at him gratefully.

'What a resourceful man you are, Richard; prepared for all eventualities!'

'I try to be.' He glanced at his watch. 'If you're ready I think we ought to press on. You might like to sleep a little. Lean back and close your eyes.'

Harriet was not at all happy to sleep away her remaining time with Richard, but her lids felt like lead as she turned her head to look at his profile as he drove back to rejoin the main highway. He looked abstracted, lost in his own thoughts, and seemed disinclined for conversation.

'Thank you for driving me to Lisbon,' she said drowsily 'you were quite right. I've enjoyed the trip much more in the car.'

He gave her a musing, oddly melancholy look before looking straight ahead once more. 'The journey isn't over yet. Try to sleep for a while.'

Harriet watched him for a time, trying to imprint his profile on her memory for afterwards, but very soon the heat of the afternoon and her filling meal got the better of her and she slumped in her seat in a dead sleep, her hair rivalling the sunlight in a bright splash of colour against the buff upholstery of the car.

She had great trouble in trying to wake up. There seemed to be weights on her eyelids, and her head felt full of something resembling hot cotton wool that shifted continuously in a rolling motion that decided her against even attempting to make the effort for a while. It seemed most unfair to feel queasy like this. She had refused wine with her lunch, keeping to mineral water because she was travelling, and after the meal there had only been the fruit juice drunk in the car.

Car! The realisation struck her like a missile and she shot upright, her dark eyes wide open. They widened even more as she stared, horrified, at her surroundings.

For one thing she was no longer in a car. She fought for calm as she tried to assimilate one fact at a time. Nauseated and trembling she raised herself with effort against hard, aromatic-smelling pillows and leaned against them weakly, breathing rapidly, as she tried to reason out where on earth she could be. The room was high-ceilinged and bare, and the four-poster bed she lay in dominated it. The walls of the room were a faded green, with plaster crumbling into scabrous patches here and there, the colour only just discernible in the gloomy light filtering through two dust-coated windows which flanked a door of bare, louvred wood. Apart from the bed there was only a rattan chair, a rickety bedside table and a marble-topped wash-stand decorated with vivid tiles, with a damp-spotted ornate mirror above it. There were no pictures on the walls, only a crucifix in black wood carved so skilfully the agony of the Christ figure leapt out at Harriet, and she swallowed hard and raised a hand to her damp forehead. She stared at her arm, then down at herself. She was enveloped in a shroud-like garment of white linen, hand-woven and soft with age, trimmed with lace at the wrists and across the breasts below a high collar. She was lying in the exact middle of the large bed, which had a canopy of yellowed white fabric, fraying at the edges, but the counterpane spread neatly over her was blazingly clean, linen again with inserts of lace which had words worked in it. The room smelt of dust and age and had an overpowering air of neglect and decay, and the floor was bare with unpolished boards that struck cold through the soles of her feet as she swung them gingerly to the ground. Her head swam alarmingly, and she sat, trembling, beads of perspiration on her forehead, until the room was still again, then she rose unsteadily to her feet and made slowly for the door.

She was surprised to find it swung open with a creak as she turned the handle, almost sure she would have been locked in. There was no sound of people talking, or passing traffic, or any life at all as she crept cautiously outside on to what proved to be a verandah running the entire length of a long, one-storey building. There were other doors, flanked by windows like the room Harriet had just left, in a row along the verandah, but they were closed, the windows blank, and she moved to the edge of the verandah and clutched weakly at the bare wood of the rail as her starting eyes took in the scene below her. For one thing it was early morning. Which morning? she wondered. It had been afternoon when she fell asleep in the car, but who was to say if this were the next day, or the next week, or some other time altogether? Perhaps she was in some time-warp, and had been spirited to another century. It felt like it as she gazed at a landscape which looked like something from another world. She could see a valley deeply cleft by a river rushing down through it between steep crags, with lower slopes covered in a wild carpet of vegetation. She forced herself to try and identify it, and thought she could make out broom, gorse, ferns, oaks and other trees she thought might be chestnut, but nowhere amongst it all was any sign of habitation or another human being. Nearer at hand there was a wide path of hard-packed earth around the building, which appeared to be very big and very decrepit and only one step from being overtaken by the encroaching vegetation. The rust-red tiles of the roof were cracked, some of them missing in places, and the walls had once been white, but now were dusty and crumbling, and the woodwork everywhere was stripped clean of any paint. In one direction Harriet could see another structure forming a T with the main house, and she stiffened as she heard sounds coming from it.

Feeling vulnerable and incredibly silly in the voluminous nightgown, she crept warily along the verandah towards the rear section, smothering a scream as a large cockroach scuttled across her path. She stopped, shivering, only now coming alive to the fact that she was cold, the air was cold, and she had nothing on beneath her incredible garment, which covered her more than adequately from throat to ankle, it was true, but did nothing much in the way of keeping her warm. But yesterday—if it *had* been yesterday—the weather had been warm. Jolted out of her fear, Harriet narrowed her dark eyes in anger. Richard Livesey must have brought her to this terrible, beautiful place. But why?

Stung into action, she pulled herself together and went along the verandah, bursting through the door of the room crosswise at the end of it. She stopped dead inside the doorway, speechless. She was in a great cavern of a room with a fire burning in an enormous hearth where an old woman dressed in black stirred a cauldron suspended by a chain over the flames, looking so like one of the witches from *Macbeth* Harriet was seized with an overwhelming desire to giggle as the woman, oblivious to her presence, went on stirring the pot with a huge wooden spoon with a carved handle. A long scrubbed table stood in the middle of the room, with benches either side and a wicker chair with carved wooden arms at the head of it. Garlands of garlic hung from the blackened beams of the ceiling, and Harriet gave them a wry look, wondering if their purpose was purely culinary, or if they were kept as protection from vampires.

She took in a deep breath and marched across the big, shadowy room to tap the old woman on the shoulder. 'Excuse me,' she said politely, 'but could you please tell me where I am?'

The woman spun round and stared aghast at the wild-haired apparition confronting her, a torrent of incomprehensible words issuing from a face as brown and wrinkled as a walnut beneath the black kerchief tied over her head.

'You don't speak English,' said Harriet in dismay, and the woman put a hand behind her ear, miming that she was unable to hear. 'And you're deaf too,' added Harriet hopelessly, and shivered again.

The woman pulled the rattan chair towards the fire and pushed the girl down into it, picking up a black wool shawl from the bench to wrap around Harriet's shoulders, indicating that she should stretch out her feet to the blaze. Harriet did so gratefully, then watched avidly as the old woman poured coffee from a battered metal pot into a blue china cup and added sugar from a bowl on the table. There was milk frothing in a pan close to the fire, and the woman poured a little into the cup and handed it to her, a gap-toothed smile lighting her face as Harriet mimed her fervent thanks and drank thirstily. The coffee was pure nectar, strong and fresh and quite the best she'd ever tasted. When her cup was empty the old woman fetched a plate with a chunk of corn bread and a portion of creamy cheese, and Harriet tried her best to eat a little, but her stomach still felt fragile and she left most of it, though she drank eagerly when the woman refilled her coffee-cup.

Afterwards the woman tactfully conducted her to the very primitive sanitary arrangements, which apparently served the entire house, then escorted her along the verandah and helped her back into bed, overriding the girl's protests with repeated sentences of disagreement in which Harriet was sure she could make out the words

'Dom Ricardo' several times. In the end it was easiest to give in. She felt distinctly ropey anyway, and bed was probably the best place when there was no sign of her clothes, or of any of her belongings. With difficulty she managed to make the woman understand that she would prefer the bedroom left open to let the maximum of light into the room, then she was left to her own devices in the great carved bed.

Harriet had no idea how long it was, but lying there with nothing to do but pore over her predicament it seemed like hours and hours before the sound of a horse's hoofs outside on the hard earth brought her bolt upright against the hard, lace-edged pillows. Heavy footsteps tramped along the verandah and a moment later a man appeared in the doorway, his back to the light as he advanced slowly into the room. Spurs on his knee-length boots clanked with every step, and he stood looking down at her in silence as he took off a broad-brimmed black felt hat. Harriet gazed at him speechlessly, at the great sheepskin jerkin he wore over a rough homespun shirt and thick dark breeches. He stripped off rubbed leather gloves and subjected her to a hard, cold scrutiny very different from the look directed at her over the lunch table in Alcacer do Sal.

'Good morning,' said Richard Livesey slowly, and drew the gloves through his hands with a flicking motion. 'I trust I find you well?'

Any faint hope Harriet had nurtured about this all being some horrible mistake died a painful death as she returned his look steadily.

'Dom Ricardo, I presume,' she said flatly.

'That's how I'm known here.'

'Do you have a number of aliases?'

'No. My only name is Richard Livesey. Old Isabel uses the Portuguese equivalent—or sometimes "*Patrao*"—to make things clearer to you.'

'Clearer to me?' Harriet's eyes flashed dark fire in her pale face. 'Nothing is clear to me! Where is this place?

Why am I here?'

'To bring about the fulfilment of one of your ambitions,' he said, astounding her.

'I have no idea what you're talking about.' She glared at him in resentment. 'I demand you give me my clothes and my belongings before you explain yourself!' She was hard put to keep the lump in her throat from choking her. To think she had trusted herself to this man, had almost—almost—she cringed as she remembered the way he had let him make love to her the other night.

'I'll have Isabel bring your things to you right away,' he said. 'She has laundered the clothes you wore in the car. I'm afraid she was unable to explain. She speaks only Portuguese, and she's also quite deaf.'

'That much I've learned for myself. She was very kind to me, even so.' Suddenly Harriet lost her temper completely. 'But I don't know why I'm talking to you so reasonably when I've been virtually kidnapped and presumably drugged to make me sleep so long. God, what a fool I was! You actually conned me into believing you wanted me along on the car trip for the pleasure of my company!' She threw back her head and met his indifferent blue eyes with a look of loathing. 'You took me in so easily. I even laughed when the Armstrongs joked about white-slave-traffickers.' She gave an uneven little laugh. 'They agreed with me that you didn't look the part, but they should see you now, Dom Ricardo! *Is* that what you intend to do? Sell me off to the highest bidder? I've heard that my colouring goes down well in some parts of the world.' She laughed again and went on laughing, and found she couldn't stop, and with a muttered oath Richard slapped her cheek sharply and the laughter changed to tears. Appalled by her own lack of self-control, Harriet turned her head into the pillows and wept behind a tangled veil of hair which concealed her face from the man watching her.

Without a word he strode from the room, the sound of his spurred boots on the bare boards penetrating her misery, and she looked up, scrambling up from the bed to run after him, wanting to demand an explanation, and insist that he took her back to the hotel. She was brought to a skidding standstill by the sight of her own reflection in the spotted mirror on the wall. It might be as well to do something about her appearance before she saw Richard Livesey, or anyone else for that matter again. Then something struck her. She must have been missed by now. The courier, Manoel, would have expected her at the hotel in Lisbon. She brightened. Richard would be forced to take her back—he couldn't keep her here against her will. This was the twentieth century, not the Middle Ages. She whirled round as the door opened, but it was only old Isabel, who came in with Harriet's clothes folded carefully over her arm, also a towel and some soap. She held them out with a smile and said something rapid in which '*patrao*' was the only word Harriet recognised.

'*Obrigado*,' said Harriet loudly, remembering the word for thank you from her Portuguese phrase book, and Isabel gave her a wide, delighted smile in response before hurrying from the room, miming that she would return at once. This time she brought a pail of steaming water and poured it into the big pottery basin on the washstand, then she went out again, closing the door firmly behind her. Harriet yearned to lock it, but there was no key, so she dragged the chair against the door and rammed the back of it under the handle, and only then stripped off the tent-like nightgown and laid it on the bed.

Shivering, she washed herself all over with the strong-smelling soap, and rubbed herself dry briskly before putting on the clothes she had chosen for the journey. It seemed a very long time since she had dressed in them in her hotel bedroom in such eager anticipation. She smiled bitterly. Perhaps it *was* a long time. Her watch was missing, and she had no way of telling how long she had lain in that bed in a drugged sleep. She was certain Richard *had* drugged her. Her head still felt muzzy, and her tongue and mouth felt rough and dry, and thoughts of Isabel's coffee began to tantalise her.

The door handle rattled against the chair as someone tried to come in and she stiffened, but it was Isabel's voice that called '*senhora*', and feeling rather silly Harriet pulled the chair away and let the old woman in. Isabel eyed the chair with approval, giving Harriet a wise smile as she handed over a coarse-toothed comb. Harriet smiled radiantly and turned away to the mirror, dragging the comb through her hair ruthlessly, ignoring the knots in it as she raked the tangles from the dishevelled mane. Diffidently Isabel took two ornamental combs from her apron pocket and offered them to Harriet, who thanked her gratefully as she secured her hair behind her ears with the combs, which were of tortoiseshell and decorated with a row of tiny gold filigree hearts. Isabel was busy restoring the great bed to pristine order when Harriet touched her shoulder gently, saying '*Dom Ricardo*' slowly and distinctly when the woman turned to face her. By much gesturing and mime Harriet was able to make the woman understand she wanted to see Richard, and Isabel beckoned her from the room and gestured towards the kitchen at the back of the house.

When Harriet went into the kitchen Richard Livesey was seated at the head of the table in the one chair the room possessed, his booted legs stretched in front of him as he stared sombrely into the cup of coffee on the table. He had discarded the sheepskin jerkin, but even so looked very different from the elegant, urbane man of the evening in Porches. This was a rougher, more basic male creature, not even like the shabby fisherman of that first morning, but a man with an air of implacability about him Harriet found daunting. He rose slowly to his feet as he saw her, but no smile softened the regularity of his dark features as his eyes met hers. There was no spark of warmth in the ultramarine stare. It was cold and hostile, and any last feeble flicker of hope in Harriet's heart guttered and went out, extinguished by the waves of enmity coming from the motionless man.

'I demand to know why I'm here,' she began, dispensing with social niceties. 'I would also like to know exactly where "here" is, and insist on immediate transportation back to Praia do Ceu. I'm a British citizen and you can't keep me here against my will, especially as I'll be missed at the hotel.'

The indifference on Richard's face was galling as he motioned her to a seat on one of the benches.

'You won't be missed,' he said, 'because I informed the management you'd consented to come away for a few days with me.'

Harriet went white with fury. 'You did what?' she spat.

'I think you heard me well enough.' Richard strolled over to the hearth and brought the coffee-pot to the table, pouring some of the fragrant contents into a cup and pushing it towards her.

Forcing herself to stay calm, she pushed the coffee away. 'How do I know *that* won't be drugged, as well?' she asked.

'It's not drugged,' he said coolly. 'If you like I'll drink from the cup first.'

'That would make it even less acceptable,' she retorted.

Richard shrugged, lit a cigar and leaned back in his chair, his eyes studying her through the curling smoke. 'I brought you here, as I said earlier, to help you realise an ambition, and at the same time to undergo a little punishment in return for what someone else suffered at your hands not so long ago.'

Harriet began to experience a very real fear. The man must be deranged. It was the only possible explanation. She took a deep breath to steady herself. 'I haven't the faintest idea what you mean.'

'Let me explain.' Richard got up and took a folded sheet of paper from his back pocket and tossed it across to her.

'The photograph attached to that is yours, I assume; you've made no mention of a twin sister.'

CHAPTER FOUR

HARRIET unfolded the paper and stared incredulously at the snapshot stapled to it. It was half a photograph, a shot of herself in a very brief bikini, her hair rioting wildly over her shoulders as she laughed with her companion, who had been cut off the print. Only a bare male arm across her shoulders was left of Guy, but originally they had both been laughing at Delia and telling her to get a move on with the photograph, which had been taken at least three years before in the garden at the back of Guy's cottage. Harriet turned over the snapshot and frowned at the signature 'Harry', on the back. Only Guy ever called her that, and this was not his typical doctor's scrawl, neither was it her own flowing script, though it had a vague similarity. She stole a look at Richard's watchful face, then turned her attention to the letter attached to the photograph.

'Dear Box No 1348', it began. 'I could be just the one you're looking for. I have long blonde hair with natural waves, a 37-23-35 figure and I'm 5ft 6ins tall. I've done some modelling, I adore having a really good time, and long to travel and see the world. Wouldn't you like to find out how far we can go together? If you would, reply to Box No 1521. I'll be waiting.'

The letter was typed—quite well, too, Harriet noted automatically, then read the provocative little note again before she pushed snapshot and letter back to the top of the table where Richard sat impassively.

'I suppose you deny all knowledge of this,' he said.

'Not entirely. It's my photograph, of course; taken some time ago, but I remember the occasion well,' she answered calmly.

'And the man with you, no doubt.'

'Of course.' Their eyes met and clashed and Harriet said with emphasis, 'But I have never laid eyes on that letter. I neither typed nor composed it, and I didn't sign the photograph, either. If I had it would have been "Harriet", not "Harry". And I still don't see how all this leads to my being here.'

'Allow me to explain.' Richard's sharp eyes saw her look fleetingly towards the cup of coffee. 'You have my word it hasn't been doctored.'

'Your word,' she said without inflection, and with a curse he jumped to his feet, drank the coffee down in one draught and went over to the fireplace for the coffee-pot. He filled another cup and pushed it across the table to her, then went back to his seat.

Harriet looked defiant as she stirred sugar into the coffee before sipping it. 'I consider my suspicion justified.'

Richard ignored her. 'Now,' he said, 'perhaps you'll listen while I tell you a salutary little tale about a young friend of mine; a young man I'm very fond of, and a family connection. His sister is married to my brother.'

'You have a brother?' Harriet's little smile made it plain she was surprised that her captor was normal enough to possess a family.

'Yes, I do. But he's not the subject of my discourse,' said Richard drily. 'Let me start with a young man at Oxford who is about to celebrate his birthday in style. Black tie dinner, party afterwards, music, champagne, all the trimmings, including the most sought-after girl in Oxford as his partner.'

Harriet drank her coffee in silence, watching Richard's face as he spoke, and wondering how all this could have anything to do with her. The sardonic gleam in his eye made it fairly clear he thought she was putting on an act and she glanced away, stung, as he went on.

'Our young hero had been pursuing the lady in

question for some time, but this was the first invitation she had accepted from him, and he was triumphant about it. He kept hinting to his friends about the girl he was bringing, how green with envy they'd be when they saw his sexy blonde, but keeping her identity a secret, childish in his desire to surprise. Now our hero is a tall, pretty attractive young stud himself, good at sport as well as clever, and he'd always had the pick of the crop anyway when it came to girls, so naturally his colleagues were intrigued by all the mystery. Then a couple of weeks before the big day the lady in question announces she can't make it to the party after all. I gather she had a better offer for some other, more exalted engagement, and dropped our lad like a hot brick. But now, of course, he's told everyone who'll listen that he's bringing this exciting, fabulous partner to the do, and almost frantic with disappointment, not to mention the dread of losing face, he puts an ad in the personal colums of all the commercial papers within a fifty-mile radius. You must have seen the sort of thing.'

Harriet had. She amused herself by reading it on Sunday mornings after working her way through the *Sunday Times*.

Richard's face darkened. 'At this point our young fool went a bit haywire, made his ad exaggeratedly exotic in the hope of netting a suitable fish first time. As far as I remember it was something like "attractive male, own luxury apartment and sports car, tired of usual company, seeks young curvaceous lady with view to exciting night life and exotic holidays abroad. Must be blonde, preferably actress or model." And *that*——' he stabbed a finger towards the photograph '—came in reply.'

Harriet shook her head violently. 'But I didn't send it! I don't know how your young friend came by that snapshot, but it wasn't through me!'

Richard laughed unpleasantly. 'I hardly expected you to admit it, Harriet—or do you prefer "Harry"?'

'No, I do not,' she said hotly, 'and you're making a big mistake——'

'I don't think so,' he interrupted coldly. 'Besides, I haven't finished my story. I myself was in Oxford that weekend, staying with friends, and I took the boy to lunch to celebrate his birthday. He poured out the story of his party, and the ad in the paper, and said he was meeting the lady in question off the train that evening and was grateful for my cheque as he intended using some of it to hire a car to impress her. I told him not to waste his money and offered the loan of my Lotus.'

Harriet looked up at him, surprised.

'Ring a bell?' he asked instantly.

'No. But you said you were a farmer—I thought you'd have had a Land Rover, or something.'

'Not necessarily.' Richard poured himself more coffee and drank it thirstily. 'I told the boy I'd collect it next morning, thinking he'd probably be in no fit state to drive it back himself, but when I turned up at the flat his room-mates were in a hell of a state. The boy hadn't even put in an appearance at his own party. He had been found unconscious in a crashed car—a Lotus—on the outskirts of Oxford, not far from a pub where he'd been seen drinking with a blonde girl. No one else was in the car, which mercifully didn't catch fire, but the poor young fool was reeking of drink and there was a quantity of marijuana in the car, some of it in cigarette-stubs in the ashtray. Of the lady there was no sign, except that eventually a witness turned up who'd seen someone answering to the right description running from the scene of the accident at roughly the right time. The boy was taken to the John Radcliffe hospital with a suspected fracture of the skull, broken leg, facial laceration, etc., but the woman was never traced.'

Harriet's dark eyes were wide with horror. 'But that's monstrous!' she began, then stopped dead. 'And you believe this woman is me?' she asked in disbelief.

'I do,' said Richard wearily. 'I wish to God I didn't.'

'But Richard, I swear I didn't send that photograph. It's all some ghastly mistake.' She looked at him imploringly, her empty stomach churning.

'I traced you, from the telephone number on that letter, to the mail order firm where you work. You must have been there in the car when the boy drove it into a hedge, suffering from a combination of hash and alcohol. Until that night smoking grass was not, I gather, one of his weaknesses.' His sombre eyes bored into hers.

'And you believe that I'm the type of woman who'd even answer an advertisement like that, let alone get a boy younger than myself high on drugs and drink and leave him half dead in a car when it crashed?' Harriet's face, already colourless, turned deathly white as the man watched and he leaped from his chair, ready to catch her as she swayed in her seat.

'Don't touch me,' she whispered, white to the lips, 'or I'll throw up!'

Richard Livesey's face was a mask as he witnessed Harriet's struggle with her nausea, beads of perspiration standing out on her forehead as she gradually overcame her weakness.

'The evidence was all there,' he said flatly, when she was capable of listening to him. 'The letter, the photograph, the address, are all incontrovertible proof.'

'And your young friend,' she said through stiff lips. 'What does he say?'

'He doesn't have total recall of that night, but when he looked at your photograph he was almost certain you were the one.'

'Then there's not much I can say, is there?' Harriet's eyes were dull as they met his. 'Tried and convicted as I seem to be, am I allowed to ask why you brought me here?'

'I felt partly responsible for what happened—I lent him the car,' said Richard grimly. 'So I promised my sister-in-law, who is more than fond of her baby brother, that as his family didn't want the case brought to court

I'd do my best to trace the mysterious blonde myself and contrive some sort of punishment to fit the crime.'

'You were very lucky I happened to be coming to the Algarve at this time,' said Harriet bitterly.

'There was no luck about it, my dear. I paid for the holiday, and I also reimbursed your Mr Jackson with a generous sum for entering into the spirit of things. He fondly believes I'm madly in love with his beautiful secretary, and wasn't too hard to bribe into letting you have the time off. At this moment he's probably picturing you and me in an idyllic interlude of unbridled passion in sunny Portugal.' Richard's voice held a cutting note that wounded Harriet like a knife-thrust.

'So why did you bring me here to this wilderness?' she asked bitterly at last, after a long interval of trying to take in his story.

'Ah, but first I provided the good time advertised, a little nightlife in the Algarve, and now I'm furnishing the exotic location also promised. I thought a few days in the remotest part of Minho, living life as it used to be, would be an amusingly punitive experience for a fun-loving blonde. A complete change, as it were. No alcohol, unfamiliar food, primitive sanitary arrangements, no entertainment—I thought it would be interesting to watch you cope with it all.'

They stared at each other, their eyes locked in silent combat.

'Didn't the hotel people think it odd, my taking off into the blue with you on such short acquaintance?' asked Harriet.

'Possibly.' Richard gave her a sardonic smile. 'But they believe you came willingly, happily even, witnessed by both Manoel Pires and the receptionist. They'll simply think you're one of those sociable ladies who seize whatever chances of diversion are offered them.'

'And the Armstrongs?' she asked, feeling sick again.

'They would have been given a message too, don't

worry.' His eyes sharpened. 'Do you feel faint again—Harriet——?'

Without answering she fled from the room to the primitive water closet, where she retched miserably, her empty stomach protesting as she tried to rid it of its non-existent contents. Eyes streaming and gasping for breath, she went outside into the sunlight, shivering a little.

'Are you better?' Richard put a hand out towards her as she wavered on her feet a little.

'Better than what?' she snapped, and shied away from his touch. 'I *said* don't touch me—or does this amusing punishment of yours include a spot of "*droit de seigneur*"?'

'Don't put ideas in my head,' he retorted, then stood looming over her, hands on hips as he scrutinised her green-white face. 'Though at the moment you're hardly a sight to inspire raging lust.'

'And whose fault is that! How am I supposed to look after being given some kind of filthy knock-out drops?'

'It was a fairly harmless sleeping-draught I put in the fruit juice,' he said, sounding rather bored, to her fury. 'If you still feel any ill-effects you'd better lie down for a while.'

It seemed useless to protest that it was his sickening little story that had turned her stomach, not his sleeping-draught, and Harriet walked unsteadily towards the bedroom. She paused at the door and looked at him wearily. 'I suppose it *was* only yesterday you brought me here?'

'Of course.' He looked at her curiously. 'Why?'

'It seems such a long time ago,' she said bleakly, and went inside the room, closing the door carefully behind her. She had no desire for sunlight now. She wanted darkness and privacy to lick the wounds inflicted by Richard Livesey with such merciless lack of justice.

She took off her skirt and sweater, took the combs from her hair and crept back into the wide bed like a child seeking comfort in its mother's arms. Dry-eyed and miserable, she turned her back to the door and tried to sleep, but all the accusations Richard had made kept hitting her like arrows. And she'd thought he was falling in love with her! What a moron she could be when she really put her mind to it! The cock-and- bull story he had told her was a pack of lies as far as she was concerned— and she'd very much like to meet the young victim, if it came to that. Perhaps he was covering up his own transgressions by lying about the woman with him. Then she sighed, baffled. It still didn't explain how her photograph came to be sent in answer to an ad in the local rag. She went over and over it in her head until she was frantic, wearing herself out until nature took over and she fell into a deep natural sleep that lasted several hours, and was broken only because someone was hammering on the door.

'Harriet!' roared Richard. 'Are you all right?'

She rubbed her eyes sleepily and sat up as he strode into the room. 'What's the matter?' she asked, yawning, and hugged the covers to her chest.

'Isabel has been in to see you twice and she was becoming concerned. You were so still she grew frightened.' He stood at the carved footboard, examining her face. 'You haven't eaten anything and it's almost dinner-time. It's time to get up.' The rugged peasant in the rough clothes had been replaced by a man more like the Richard Livesey Harriet had fondly believed she had known. He wore a jerkin, it was true, but it was a heavy suede affair over a cream shirt of fine wool and corduroy trousers.

'Yes, sir, at once, sir—but I hope you'll overlook it if I don't dress for dinner.' She glared at him malevolently. 'My luggage has been confiscated.'

Richard jerked his head to the corner of the room which someone, Isabel no doubt, had lit with several candles in heavy copper holders. 'Your belongings are now on the chair over there, including your watch.'

'Thank you.' Harriet turned her head away pointedly

and waited for him to leave, and after an awkward moment or two he turned on his heel. At the door he said brusquely, 'Dinner's ready when you are.'

'Where do we eat?'

'In the kitchen. Apart from bedrooms it's the only room in the house. When the family lived here it was the centre of family life.'

'And who lives here now?' She turned to look at him curiously.

'For the time being just you and I, Harriet Neil,' he said, with a rather unnerving glint of smile.

'And Isabel!'

'Isabel has left for the night.' Richard smiled again and left, closing the door behind him with exaggerated care.

Harriet was flattened by the news. Somehow she had expected Isabel to sleep in the house at night too, and felt utterly bereft by her absence. Which was nonsense, she told herself. A deaf, elderly woman was very little protection, nevertheless Isabel was kind and her presence had been comforting. Harriet told herself not to be so wet and got out of bed to inspect the contents of her bag. The jersey dress she had packed for dining in Lisbon was happily uncrushable and emerged in reasonable shape. She smoothed its smoke-grey folds over her hips and tied the soft kid belt at the waist, thankful to have her own hairbrush to tame her hair again, and braided it severely, winding the rope into a coil on her neck and securing it with the heavy gilt pins kept in their own little silk bag in her grip. Stockings and high-heeled grey suede shoes gave her an odd sort of comfort, bringing a tinge of normality to this strange, frightening situation. Otherwise she left her face to its own devices, in no mood to make herself prettier for this wrong-headed host of hers. If he wanted to mete out some kind of rough justice he would find Harriet Neil could take most things on the chin without whining, but she was damned if she was going to make herself glamorous for him as a bonus.

Richard was lounging in a cane chair near the

enormous fireplace, and stood up as she went into the kitchen. Oil lamps and candles stood at various points, but even so the cavernous room was shadowy.

'You look better,' he commented, and waved her to a place at the table. Instead of the wooden bench a second cane chair was waiting for Harriet, to her amusement. Her punishment apparently didn't include sitting uncomfortably all evening.

'Thank you,' she said with formality, and sat down. The table was laid for two, with thick white china and battered silver cutlery, also two exquisite glass goblets, looking out of place in their surroundings. A platter of yellow corn bread, a dish of curd cheese and a flagon of wine were the only edibles in sight, but the air was fragrant with the savoury smells coming from two big pots bubbling on the fire, and to Harriet's mortification her stomach gave a very audible rumble. For the first time since their arrival Richard smiled faintly.

'You must be hungry. Isabel tells me you haven't eaten anything.'

She looked him in the eye. 'My stomach has taken rather a time to get over the after-affects of the—journey.'

'Then you'd better eat well now,' he said blandly. 'Isabel has left soup and a main meal for us. Perhaps you'd start serving.'

So she was to play serf. Harriet's mouth tightened and Richard leaned back in his chair, obviously ready to enjoy her protests. With effort she kept calm, picked up two soup plates and went over to the fireplace to inspect the contents of the smaller pot.

'Is this our first course?' she asked.

'*Caldo verde*—speciality of the Minho,' he answered. 'I hope you like it.'

Which probably means he hopes I won't, thought Harriet, and ladled a serving of hot soup into each bowl. With ceremony she placed her host's in front of him, ignoring his gracious inclination of the head in acknowledgement, and returned to the hearth for her own.

They began eating in silence. Harriet's sheer hunger overcame any hesitancy she might have felt towards the soup, which was some kind of potato broth full of shredded cabbage and floating with slices of smoked, peppery sausage, and to her surprise she quite liked it and ate with gusto, though she refused the corn bread Richard offered.

'You don't care for *pao de broa*?' he asked perfunctorily. 'It's maize bread.'

'I'm sure it's delicious, but I don't want to blunt my appetite for the next course.' Harriet got up to take their plates, quick to do so before he had the chance to give her any orders. She took the plates to the big sink at the far end of the room and left them on the stone draining-board, noting that there was only one tap, which meant only cold water. She made a mental note to see that the great iron kettle hanging over the fire was kept filled at all times, and took a look inside the other pot. She bit her lip, almost recoiling from the robust odour as she lifted the lid. The aromatic contents had far less appeal than the soup, but she would eat them if it killed her. She ladled a large helping on one plate and placed it before Richard with finicking care, then served herself with as modest a portion as possible, and proceeded to try to get the rich, highly-flavoured food down. It was an enormous effort, she found, but the sparkling wine Richard poured into her goblet was a boon in helping the meal along.

'I thought you'd put a ban on alcohol as far as I was concerned,' she observed.

'I don't regard wine as alcohol.' Richard drank some and gave her a sardonic look as he noted her struggle with the meal. 'Besides, I could hardly have indulged myself with wine if you weren't allowed any.'

Harriet's eyebrows rose. 'I doubt that my enforced abstinence would have affected your own enjoyment.'

'Which only shows how little you know me.'

'True. But don't bother to enlighten me. I've no wish to complete my education on that particular subject.'

After that there was silence while Harriet continued her battle with the indigestible stew which, to her annoyance, Richard ate with every appearance of enjoyment and even munched on corn bread spread with cheese as an accompaniment. Eventually he glanced over at her plate, which was still half full.

'You don't care for Portuguese cuisine?' he asked, and refilled her empty glass.

'I do, very much.' Harriet applied herself to the congealing remains of her meal. 'I shouldn't have eaten so much soup first, though.'

'You look as though you could do with some nourishment,' he remarked. 'You're very pale—your layer of suntan seems to have disappeared.'

She gave him a withering look. 'It had hardly been given time to establish itself before I was whisked away from any sun. I've hardly seen the light of day for two days.' She swallowed the last mouthful of her dinner and drank the rest of her wine with relief.

'Would you like a little more *chispalhada*?' There was a glint in Richard's eye.

'No, thank you; delicious, but very filling. What did you call it?'

'*Chispalhada*.' His face completely deadpan, he added, 'It's a mixture of beans, cabbage, bacon and blood sausage stewed with pigs' trotters.'

Harriet's stomach gave a lurch. 'How interesting,' she said lightly. 'I don't believe I've ever eaten pigs' trotters before.' And never will again, she vowed silently.

'There isn't a dessert, I'm afraid.'

'What, no nuns' tummies? How disappointing!' She collected the plates and unhooked the kettle from the bar over the fire. 'I'll wash up before I make coffee, if you don't mind.'

'I've already made it. It's keeping hot at the side of the fire.'

Applause, applause, thought Harriet, and wrapped herself in a rough towel before attacking the plates with a bar of hard, marbled soap which seemed to be the only available aid to dishwashing. She plunged her hands into the hot water and washed the cutlery and china vigorously with a piece of flannel, then dried them with Isabel's snowy cloth and put them back on the table. Richard had filled two cups with fragrant hot coffee and she took off her makeshift apron and sat down, wondering what the rest of the evening held in store. She looked at Richard, who sat watching her through the smoke of his cigar.

'Will you at least tell me where we are,' she said without beating about the bush, 'and just how long you intend to keep me here?'

'I shall take you back to the Miramar in good time for the flight back to England.' He got up and tapped his cigar ash into the fire, then brought over the coffee-pot and refilled her cup.' As to location—have you any idea where this is?'

Harriet shook her head. 'None whatever, except that presumably we must still be in Portugal.'

'Of course. Nowhere is very far from anywhere in Portugal.' He stretched out, relaxed, in the chair and stared into the fire. 'We're in one of the group of littoral districts in the north of Portugal known as the Minho, and this is the district of Braga. We're actually only an hour or so by car from the town of Braga itself, nevertheless this valley, and the others up here on the Cavado river, are still pretty wild and untamed. The mountain peaks you can see out there are part of the Serra do Geres, and there are some villages further north still which are quite primitive, virtually inaccessible, and haven't changed much since the Iron Age.'

Harriet looked at him thoughtfully. 'By telling me where we are aren't you afraid I'll try to get away?'

'You could try. But without passport, money, transport or any knowledge of the language and terrain I hardly think you'd get far.'

'Does this mean I'm to be confined to the house all the time I'm here?'

Richard turned his head and studied her face for a time. 'I had intended that,' he conceded. 'But if you promise to behave yourself I'll take you out riding tomorrow—if you can ride, that is.'

'Yes, I can.' Harriet's equestrian experience was confined to six lessons at the local riding-school when she was seven, but she was determined to take on any mount Richard Livesey offered if it meant escape from the creepy bedroom for a while. Her head came up haughtily. 'But I resent the reference to doubtful behaviour. Are you afraid I'll corrupt *you* as I'm supposed to have done with this young friend of yours?'

'That wasn't the sort of behaviour I meant. I'm too old and too wary to fall for any tricks of the man/woman variety. Escape is what I had in mind. Strictly forbidden.'

'Forbidden!'

'Exactly. *I* forbid it. This is a chauvinistic society in this neck of the woods, and I advise you strongly not to forget it.' Richard went over to a cupboard, coming back with a bottle and two glasses. 'Care for some *medronho*?' he said, to her surprise.

'You mean I'm allowed *medronho* too?' she asked acidly, smarting from his high-handed instructions.

'As I said before, I find it difficult to drink alone.'

'Very well,' she said carelessly. 'It should keep out the cold, if nothing else.'

Richard's black brows rose as he filled the narrow glasses. 'If you find your bed cold I have no objection to sharing it as a means of avoiding hypothermia.'

Harriet's eyes burned in her pale face. 'I'd freeze first.'

He shrugged. 'You probably will. It gets cold at night here at this time of the year.'

'I survived last night.' She drank down the spirit, following it with the coffee the way he'd shown her in

Porches, but this time there was no choking, or gasping. She hardly noticed the fiery bite of the spirit in her anger. 'How many days—and nights—do you intend to keep me prisoner?' she demanded.

'As many as I think fit.'

'You promised to take me back to Praia do Ceu in time for the flight home!'

'And I shall. I haven't decided yet just how soon I'll do so.' He yawned a little and stretched indolently in his chair. 'Depends on how soon I get bored with playing gaoler, I suppose.'

This was too much for Harriet. 'If you'll excuse me I'll go to my room,' she said with dignity.

'Take one of these candlesticks with you,' he said. 'We don't run to luxuries like electric light, I'm afraid.'

Harriet was not normally of a nervous disposition, but the walk back along the verandah in the darkness to that far-from-cosy bedroom all on her own was suddenly beyond her. She got to her feet and with the utmost reluctance forced herself to smile at Richard.

'Would you mind walking back to my room with me?' she said in a stifled voice.

'Afraid of the dark?'

The mockery in his voice stung and she retorted. 'Spiders and beetles, actually. But don't disturb yourself if it's too much trouble. I dare say I'll manage on my own.' She snatched up the candlestick and marched from the room, shielding the flame with her hand, but Richard was at her heels as she reached her door, one of the oil-lamps held high to light her way.

Harriet cast him a hostile look and entered the bedroom warily, setting down the candlestick on the marble top of the washstand. She watched anxiously as he directed the light towards the shadowy corners of the room with an irritating air of forbearance.

'All clear, as far as I can tell,' he pronounced.

Harriet eyed his oil-lamp covetously. 'Will you leave that with me, please?' It went against the grain to ask

favours, but by night the bedroom had even less appeal
than in daylight, and the thought of being alone there
with only a candle gave her the creeps. Richard set the
lamp on a small table near the bed.

'You didn't strike me as the type to be afraid of the
dark,' he said, amused.

Harriet's eyes flashed. 'You know nothing at all about
me. And what you *think* you know is utterly, utterly
wrong. All this is a ghastly mistake—I never went to
Oxford to answer any stupid advertisement, and I most
certainly am not the woman who was with your friend in
your Lotus. I don't *need* to answer ads to get escorts,
Richard Livesey, if that *is* your name. I don't suffer from
a lack of male company—ever!'

In the wavering, shadowy light Richard Livesey's face
looked as hard and dark as the wood the huge bed was
carved from. 'I'm afraid you'll have to do without it
tonight,' he said harshly, and strode from the room.

Harriet watched the door slam shut behind him, her
nails cutting half moons in the palms of her clenched
hands as she fought for self-control. In despair she sank
down on the bed, staring unseeingly at the bare boards of
the floor. This was all so unreal. It just couldn't be
happening. If only she could get to sleep perhaps
tomorrow she would wake to find she had been dreaming
and she was back in the hotel room at the Miramar and
Richard Livesey was just a figment of her imagination.
She laughed joylessly. If only he were! That was the worst
of it, of course. Not the fact that he'd virtually kidnapped
her and brought her to this extraordinary place, but that
he'd deliberately set out to attract and disarm her, delude
her into thinking he was falling in love with her, even to
the point of actually making love to her that last night.
Harriet's face burned. How he must have enjoyed
making her respond, she thought viciously; revelled in
breaking down her defences almost to the point of no
return. She squirmed with self-loathing and flung off the
bed to rummage in her bag for the two paperback novels

brought to read on the return coach trip that never was, as far as she was concerned. She searched impatiently, then turned out her bag, but in vain. The high and mighty Dom Ricardo must have confiscated them. It was the last straw! After sleeping so much during the day she felt only too wide-awake, and the idea of tossing and turning in that museum piece of a bed without anything to read was insupportable. She snatched up the candlestick and stormed along the verandah to the kitchen to find Richard morosely contemplating the contents of a balloon glass full of brandy. He looked up with a sardonic lift of eyebrow as she stalked across the room.

'What is it this time, Harriet? No electric blanket? No television set? What creature comfort have I failed to supply?' His voice acted on her like a goad.

'I'm not asking you to *supply* anything,' she bit out, holding her temper on a perilously short rein. 'I'm simply requesting the return of my own property.'

Richard shook his head, unmoved. 'I keep your money, your passport, your traveller's cheques—just in case you have any romantic ideas about flight. You get them back when we return to the Algarve.'

'I am not so lacking in intelligence that I even contemplated asking for the return of those! I want the books that were in my bag.'

'Sorry. You can't have those, either.'

Harriet glared at him. 'Why not?' she demanded.

'That would be spoiling you too much. The women who lived here had no leisure to sit around reading, my dear. They cooked and embroidered and prayed and set themselves to pleasing their man at the end of the day. That bed you're occupying is the *cama de matrimonio*— the marriage bed. Reading was not one of the activities expected to occur in it.' The steely challenge in his eyes slowly changed to deep appreciation of the hectic colour staining her cheeks as she stared back at him in silent fury as he got slowly to his feet.

Suddenly all the fear and anger and mortification of

this exhausting day boiled up inside Harriet like an upsurge of lava in a volcano. Without warning she let fly at the dark, taunting face above her, catching Richard squarely across the jaw with all the power she could muster. Her hand struck him so hard her palm stung badly, but she exulted in the pain as she whirled round and ran from the room. The memory of his angry outrage was a delightful balm for the wounds the day had inflicted, and once inside her bedroom filled her with the energy to drag the washstand against the closed door. Brushing her hands together in satisfaction, she undressed and climbed in the wide bed. She left the oil-lamp burning for company, though now the door was secure against invaders of any kind she felt oddly relaxed. Hitting out at Richard Livesey had relieved her pent-up emotions considerably, and even without a book to read she settled down fairly peaceably, and was almost asleep when a knock on the door jolted her out of her drowsiness to the sound of Richard's voice outside.

'Harriet,' he called. 'Harriet, may I come in?'

Might he come in indeed! Harriet turned on her stomach and let him knock, hoping he would bruise his knuckles in the process. She listened as he rattled the doorknob, chuckling silently in fierce satisfaction as he cursed audibly when the door met obstruction.

'Harriet!' he roared. 'Let me in! You can't be asleep.'

Which was true enough, she conceded, considering the row he was making. She slid out of bed and very deliberately turned out the lamp before getting back under the covers. That should get the message through, she thought smugly, and lay relaxed as Richard knocked again twice before finally retreating along the verandah. Somehow the darkness was not nearly as menacing as she had expected. The moon had risen and the room was relatively light, and with a sigh she snuggled into the resistant pillow as much as she could and went off to sleep as easily as if this were the end of any ordinary working day.

CHAPTER FIVE

WHEN Harriet woke up next morning she had no trouble in identifying her surroundings, even managing a smile at the thought that her sleeping quarters could hardly be confused with any other she had ever occupied before. Light was percolating through the windows; pale, early light, and she slid out of bed to wrestle the washstand back to its usual place before opening the door to gaze out at the beautiful, wild landscape descending so abruptly from the immediate surroundings of the house, which was situated at the summit of a hill as far as she could make out. She ventured cautiously outside the door, shivering as she stubbed her bare toes on something lying outside. Her books lay on the boards, and she eyed them for a moment before picking them up. So they were the reason for Richard's visit the night before! She took them back inside the room, smiling a little sheepishly. Somehow she had been wholly convinced that retaliation had been Richard's sole object in coming to her room.

Which only showed how mistaken one could be about someone, she reflected as she dressed hurriedly in her white shirt and sweater, plus the jeans she always included in her luggage wherever she went just in case they were necessary. These were pale blue, admittedly, but they would do if Richard really did mean to take her riding. After last night's little episode, of course, she might be confined to quarters since he was so keen on punishment to fit the crime. Harriet shrugged, less dismayed by the prospect than she would have been the day before. Then the after-effects of the sleeping-draught had still been in her system, distorting the situation and rendering her more vulnerable to the predicament in which fate—in the shape of Richard Livesey—had landed her. Now she was more her usual self, and she eyed her reflection in the spotted mirror, pleased to see her eyes looked less like two burned holes in a blanket this morning. In fact they positively sparkled with vitality after such a good night's rest, their dark brilliance providing their usual striking contrast with the bright gold of her hair, which proved more than usually difficult to get under control as she attacked it militantly with a hairbrush. Ruthlessly she pushed it behind her ears and secured it with Isabel's combs before plaiting it into a loose braid to keep it out of the way, then she made her bed, tidied the room and went along to the kitchen where Isabel was already at work. Steam was coming from the huge iron kettle over the fire, which had obviously been banked overnight and replenished with logs this morning. The poor woman must have been hard at it since dawn, thought Harriet, and gave her a bright smile of greeting as she ventured '*Bom dia*' very loudly, hoping she had said it correctly. From Isabel's delighted look she had not only heard but understood Harriet's greeting, and somehow managed to convey that the visitor looked much better, asking, by miming with her hands folded under chin, if the *senhora* had slept well.

Harriet nodded vigorously and sat down near the fire where Isabel indicated, feeling guilty at letting the old woman wait on her, but sensing that Isabel would be upset if she protested. This time the corn bread and cheese tasted as marvellous as the coffee, and Harriet ate and drank with an enthusiasm that won Isabel's warm approval. She was finishing her second cup of coffee by the time the clanking of spurs heralded Richard's arrival, and she looked at him warily as he came into the room in the clothes of the previous afternoon. The boots and breeches and thick wool shirt were all heavy and coarse and the antithesis of anything else Harriet had seen him wear, but annoyingly he looked just as much at home in the rough garb as he did in the expensive tailoring, only

more formidable still, particularly as below his cheek-
bone there were the faint but unmistakable beginnings of
a bruise, which went well with the villainous black
growth of stubble on his chin.

Harriet eyed the bruise with satisfaction and said
'Good morning' as though breakfast with a strange man
in this unknown part of the world were the most normal
thing in the world.

'Good morning,' he replied distantly, and sat at the
head of the table. '*Bom dia*,' he said, to Isabel, and smiled
at her affectionately. '*Ovos fritos, por favor*. Have *you* had
breakfast?' he added, turning to Harriet.

'Yes, thank you.'

There was a flood of Portuguese from Isabel as she
placed a large iron frying pan on the flames and poured
oil into it. Richard replied soothingly, in a manner far
removed from the one he reserved for Harriet.

'She's asking whether you'd care for the fried eggs I
asked for,' he told her. 'She's rather put out because she
had no way of asking you herself.'

Harriet jumped up and touched Isabel's shoulder,
smiling and trying to make her understand she hadn't
wanted eggs for breakfast.

'Will you tell her that in England I never eat any
breakfast at all,' she asked Richard, 'and that the coffee
she makes is the best I've ever tasted—oh, and tell her
how much I enjoyed the meal last night.'

There was a twist to Richard's expressive mouth as he
conveyed Harriet's words to the old servant, who
laughed, gratified, and became voluble again.

'She says she'll prepare another local dish today,'
translated Richard, and began to eat the eggs Isabel set
in front of him. He gave a quick, gleaming glance at
Harriet's apprehensive face as he helped himself to
bread.

'How nice,' said Harriet drily, and tried not to think of
the *chispalhada*. 'What part of the pig is on the menu
today?'

'No idea.' Richard's look of smug amusement was galling. 'Sorry you came to Portugal?' he added.

'If I am,' returned Harriet with heat, 'it's nothing to do with Isabel's cooking, nor with the country and the people. From what I've been permitted to see of it the whole country is beautiful and the people charming and friendly. In fact every prospect pleases, and only one man in particular is vile.' She bestowed a smile of such piercing sweetness on him Isabel was plainly enchanted as she set the coffee-pot down on the table.

'It's obvious you feel much better today,' he said, unmoved. 'Fighting fit, in fact—though now I come to think of it you'd arrived at the fighting stage as early as yesterday evening, as I know to my cost.' He fingered the bruise on his cheek with care.

Harriet filled their coffee-cups, and examined the bruise with clinical interest. 'I won't say I'm sorry, because I'm not. My signet ring must have caused the real damage, I think.'

'You pack quite a lethal punch.' Richard yawned a little, as though the subject bored him. 'Do you still want to come out riding?' he added, as though hoping her answer would be in the negative.

'Very much, please,' said Harriet promptly. 'Oh, and by the way, thank you for returning my books. I tripped over them this morning.'

'You could have had them last night just as easily!' His eyes gleamed cold over his cup. 'What exactly did you think I had in mind when I knocked on your door, for God's sake?'

She shrugged. 'Retaliation, perhaps.'

'You didn't seriously imagine I intended to knock you about?' There was such distaste on his face she was almost amused.

'Retaliation can take various forms,' she said colourlessly.

Richard studied her from beneath raised black brows. 'I assure you I had neither injury nor rape in mind. If anything I felt you had some justification for hitting out as you did. But as for anything else, Miss Neil, physically you leave me cold. I've no taste for charms dished out with such impartiality to all and sundry, believe me. If you were misled by that little scene after our dinner in Porches, I'm sorry. It was merely a form of insurance to influence you to make the trip in the car with me instead of in the coach. A sprat to catch a mackerel, if you like.'

Harriet's face emptied of expression and she sat perfectly still for a moment or two, then she got up and gathered up the used plates to take them to Isabel, who was washing towels in the big stone sink. The woman protested as she saw what Harriet was doing, and waved her away, her face shocked. Harriet smiled and thanked her, then left the kitchen to return to her bedroom where she picked up one of her books and sat down in the low cane chair to read it. The words on the page danced and writhed in front of her eyes, distorted by white-hot rage, but she kept on turning the pages at appropriate intervals until Richard's spurs announced his arrival. He leaned in the open doorway and looked at her.

'Aren't you coming riding?' he asked.

'No, I don't think I will after all, thank you,' she said, and returned to her book.

'Your enthusiasm for exercise disappeared very rapidly.'

'Not for the exercise, merely for you as companion *on* the exercise.'

His mouth curled. 'Put off by a few home truths, Harriet?'

'The truth seems to be something you wouldn't recognise if you fell over it,' she said flatly. 'Besides, I'm quite sure you'll enjoy going wherever you're going without my company—as I shall definitely enjoy *my* day a lot more without yours.'

Her eyes clashed coldly with his and he cursed, then turned on his spurred heel and strode away along the verandah with footsteps like drumbeats as he left the house.

Harriet let out the breath she had been holding and sat clutching the arms of her chair, trying to quell the terrible anger that bubbled inside her like a witch's brew. Gradually she began to feel better, particularly once the sound of the horse's hoofs somewhere beyond the house indicated that Richard Livesey was no long breathing the air anywhere in her vicinity. In her entire life she had never experienced such a violent emotion towards another human being, such an urge to wound, to hurt— even to kill. Richard Livesey would never know how narrowly he had escaped physical injury of some kind; he was lucky there had been no weapon to hand. Harriet seethed as she remembered that all this—this *stupidity* was some sort of vengeance for a boy who was apparently not even kin to him. Who did he think he was? God?

After a while she decided it was time she explored her surroundings now her gaoler had gone off and left her to her own devices. She frowned, wondering why he had no qualms about possible escape. If she could make her way to the nearest town ... but with no money that just wasn't possible, she remembered, instantly deflated. And in any case she had no idea where the nearest town *was*. It could be miles away, and the only shoes she had were the strappy flat sandals she had on, or the high-heeled grey suede affairs she had brought to wear with her dress. All of which Richard Livesey knew quite well, as no doubt he had gone through her belongings with a fine-tooth comb while she was out for the count on whatever drug he'd given her. At the thought Harriet's temper threatened to get the better of her again, so she hurried off to seek out Isabel.

With much mime and recourse to the little phrase book she had brought with her Harriet was able to ask the old woman if exploring the house was allowed.

'*Posso ver a casa?*' she shouted, after looking up useful phrases at the back of the book. She hoped she was

asking to see over the house and smiled radiantly as
Isabel nodded, waving an arm along the verandah in a
sweeping motion which obviously meant the visitor
could go where she liked. Harriet was surprised. She had
been quite convinced that locked doors would confront
her if she indulged her curiosity. Isabel returned to her
preparation of the day's meals, obviously happy for
Harriet to wander where she liked, and as Isabel was
without doubt acting on Richard's instructions it meant
there was no veto on exploration as far as he was
concerned, either. After only a few minutes it was quite
easy to see why. Each room was exactly like all the
others, every one possessing a door leading on to the
verandah which encircled the house. Some rooms were
empty, it was true, while others were furnished very
basically with a bed, a chair and a table, sometimes less.
One room at the end of the verandah held an expensive
suitcase, and a black nylon sponge-bag lay on the chair
near the bed, which was covered by a woven spread
similar to the one on hers, but less ornate. Otherwise the
furniture was very rickety stuff, no different from any
other room, except for the one allotted to Harriet. Why
had she been honoured with such splendour, decaying
though it was? she wondered wryly, and looked hard at
Richard's suitcase. It must surely contain her own
possessions as well as some clue to the personality of one
Richard Livesey, who was nothing like any other farmer
Harriet had ever encountered. Perhaps he was really a
spy and that one large piece of luggage contained a
transmitter for sending messages—only she had a feeling
that was probably bit out of date now the microchip was
taking over the world.

Chuckling to herself, she turned to leave, then the
sponge-bag caught her eye and she hesitated. The
temptation was too much, and after a quick look along
the verandah to check that Isabel was nowhere in sight
she unzipped the bag hurriedly and went through the
contents; razor, shaving-cream—no electricity here, of

course—an expensive French aftershave, toothpaste, nothing else. Then she saw a slight bump in a tiny pocket at one side and in triumph she pulled out two keys on a thin metal ring. Her heart began to beat rapidly as she found they fitted the suitcase. She raised the lid on neatly folded shirts and sweaters, socks, underwear—and that was the lot. Frantically she went through everything twice, but drew a blank. Even the pocket in the lid was empty. There were no papers or documents of any kind in the suitcase, his or hers, and Harriet sank back on her heels in bitter disappointment.

'These what you're searching for?'

The deep, mocking voice brought her to her feet in one motion, her colour high as she met the derision in Richard's eyes. He leaned in the doorway in the indolent way that was becoming familiar to her, a leather document-case dangling from one long, brown hand. 'Did you really think I'd leave them around for prying females to ferret out? Tut, tut, Harriet!'

'I thought you'd gone out,' she said inanely.

He laughed softly. 'Which is exactly what I meant you to think. I was fairly sure you wouldn't be able to resist going over my belongings once I was out of the way.'

Her composure had returned, and she shrugged indifferently. '*Your* belongings don't interest me in the slightest. It was my own property I was hoping to find.'

'They won't be of any use.' Richard pushed himself away from the door jamb and moved towards her. Her eyes dropped to his feet, and she saw why he had been able to creep up on her unheard. The boots and spurs were missing. 'Braga, the nearest town, is more than an hour away by car,' he went on, 'and there's only a roughish track leading from the house down the mountainside until you reach any kind of road.' He glanced down at her feet. 'Wearing those you wouldn't get far before your feet were in ribbons.' He stood directly in front of her, blocking her exit, and even without his boots he loomed tall in the room, which was tiny compared with Harriet's, but she stood her ground and looked pointedly towards the door.

'Now you've had the satisfaction of adding petty larceny to the rest of the black-list against me perhaps you'll let me pass.' Harriet stared up at him defiantly, and could have sworn for a moment there was admiration on his face before dismissing the idea impatiently. If Richard Livesey harboured any feelings about her at all admiration was hardly likely to be one of them. Her eyes fell, and she wished he would just say something, or move so she could get away; wild horses wouldn't have made her retreat, but his proximity made her uneasy. It was mortifyingly plain that loathe and despise him though she might, at the same time he still had the same powerful physical effect on her, however hard she tried to ignore it. And as if to provide tangible proof of this he took her hand in his and held it, and she felt his touch on her skin like a brand.

'I didn't come back to catch you out,' he said abruptly, and released her hand as her eyes flew to his face in surprise. 'I went only a short distance before turning back to see if I could change your mind about riding.'

'Why on earth should you do that?' Harriet found it hard to believe, and her expression showed it.

Richard shrugged. 'God knows. Let's say I'm human enough not to relish the thought of you cooped up here all day with nothing to do.'

Strong though his physical attraction might be, Harriet's suspicion of him, and his motives, was even stronger. 'I find that hard to swallow,' she said flatly, and looked down at his feet in their hand-knitted socks. 'If you're speaking the truth why did you creep around like that?'

'I thought you might be sleeping—I didn't want to disturb you.'

The sarcastic doubt in her dark eyes needed no words.

'Anyway,' she added, 'I was bragging when I said I could ride. My expertise is limited to a few lessons at a riding-school when I was a child.'

He laughed, looking immediately younger and less grim. 'Don't worry, Harriet. The mount I brought for you is a sedate old girl. Menina won't give you any trouble, I promise.'

Harriet still looked doubtful. She pointed to her feet. 'It's still not on, Richard. No boots.'

'I thought of that. Isabel has some belonging to her grandson—might be on the large side, but with a pair of my socks they should do.' He checked, eyeing her warily. 'Of course if you'd really prefer to be alone——'

'I could cut off my nose to spite myself and say yes, but I'd very much like to see something of the countryside around here,' said Harriet frankly. 'I'm not likely to get the chance again. Besides, I *had* thought I was going to see more of the Algarve. As I'm not, and it's your doing, I might as well take you up on your offer and see some of— what did you say it was called?'

'Minho. But that covers a fair-sized area. We're in a fairly remote part of it up here. So you'll come?'

'Yes.'

Richard stood aside to let her pass. 'Good, I'm glad. After all it would be a pity to spoil such a beautiful nose.'

Harriet gave him a startled, questioning look.

'I mean it,' he assured her. 'Your nose, like everything else about you, is exquisite. Physically, Harriet Neil, you leave little to be desired.'

For a moment she was sorely tempted to tell him what he could do with his compliment—and the ride—but prudence held her back. She badly wanted to see what lay beyond and below the house, and felt too full of energy to laze around all day with a book, so she summoned up a sickly sweet smile.

'Such a pity that "fair walls do oft close in pollution"— isn't it?' she said with mock regret.

Later, despite feeling rather ridiculous in one of Richard's sweaters, at his insistence, not to mention the over-large boots of Helio, Isabel's grandson, Harriet was overjoyed to be out in the fresh, clear mountain air, and not at all unhappy mounted on the placid Menina, who was a pretty little grey mare well past the first flush of youth. Richard, in contrast, sat astride a spirited chestnut several hands higher than Menina, and in his big sheepskin jerkin and broad-brimmed black felt hat looked like a brigand from an earlier time. Harriet told him so as they picked their way sedately down the steep, half-overgrown track that led downwards through woods of oak, pine and eucalyptus as they left the starker crags behind. He grinned, his teeth a flash of white in his face, which looked even darker under the hat-brim.

'Men still dress like this up here, but I suppose you're referring to my behaviour in abducting you and carrying you off to my mountain fastness. Though it rather spoils the effect by having to admit the place isn't mine.'

Harriet was beginning to get the hang of Menina's gait and was able to spare a look for her companion. He sat his horse like a man used to spending long hours in the saddle, relaxed and easy and at one with his mount.

'I'm not going to ask whose house it is,' she said drily, 'because no doubt you'll tell me in due course if you think I should know, and if you don't I'm not going to fret about it on a day like this.' She breathed in the pure air deeply, then shot him a sparkling look. 'I suppose I thought of brigands because of some vague idea about vendetta. Because that *is* what you're doing, isn't it? Wreaking vengeance on me, I mean, because of what I'm suppose to have done to this boy you talked about.'

'Vendetta?' He frowned, narrowing his eyes against the sun. 'A shade melodramatic, Harriet.'

'From where I am the whole escapade is pure melodrama from start to finish. *You* try waking in a weird, antique room you've never seen before in your life and see how melodramatic you find it, Dom Ricardo!'

Richard looked at her moodily for a moment, then dropped back a little to let her ride in front of him as the track improved. The plodding Menina picked her own way with care, leaving Harriet free to peer through the thinning trees to the deeply cleft valley below. As they gradually descended she could see man-made terraces carved out of the hillside in the distance.

'Look, Richard, over there; what are those?' She turned to look behind at Richard and saw his eyes riveted on her hair, which swung in a bright rope between her shoulder-blades. He looked away at once and followed her pointing hand.

'The terraces?' he asked. 'They call them *socalos*. Those are planted with saplings, but sometimes it's grass or tillage crops.'

'And are those vines further on down?'

He nodded and reined in Diablo, motioning Harriet to do the same with the obedient Menina. 'We're in *vinho verde* country here—Braga is the centre of the industry. The wine we drank last night came from those vineyards down there.'

'Do they actually belong to the house?' asked Harriet curiously.

'In a way. The family who own the house also own the land where the vines grow, it's true, but it's rented out to tenants who actually work on it.'

'Is this *your* family, Richard?'

'I told you my grandmother was Portuguese. The land belongs to her relatives, the Monteiros.' He slid from his horse and tethered it to a nearby tree, then did the same with Menina before holding up his arms to Harriet. She swung her legs over the saddle and descended in a rush, falling rather than sliding into his arms, and partly winding him in the process.

'You're dangerous to have around,' he said breathlessly, and set her on her feet.

'I'm not, you know. I'm perfectly harmless.' Harriet gave him a pointed little smile as she patted Menina, but to her surprise felt no real animosity at all towards Richard at this particular moment. She pulled a face and

Richard noticed it as he took a leather bag from the horse.

'What's the matter?' he asked, and gestured towards a fallen tree-trunk a little way off the track.

'I was just thinking how hard it is to hang on to my righteous indignation towards you—or anyone else— here in this wonderful pure air, and with that view down there.' Harriet shook her head. 'I must have a very high malice-threshold, or something.'

'Perhaps it's merely that out here, away from everything, most problems get cut down to size.' Richard took a bottle of wine from the bag and two bundles wrapped in the snowy cloths that were Isabel's trade-mark. 'Only crusty bread and some cheese, a few tomatoes and—yes, two oranges, plus the Monteiro wine. I hope it suits you.'

The food suited Harriet perfectly. The wine tasted like nectar, and the simple, wholesome bread and cheese were far more to her taste than the *chispalhada* of the evening before. Richard seemed to pick up her thoughts. He peeled an orange for her and head it over on the tip of the knife he took from the sheath at his belt.

'That went down much better than last night's meal, I think,' he remarked.

'Yes.' Her smile was a little sheepish. 'I'm not over-conservative in my taste in food, but frankly that was a bit much. I had quite a struggle to get it down.'

His teeth gleamed in his dark face. 'I could see that. You shouldn't have gone on eating it.'

'I wouldn't give you the satisfaction of seeing me give in.' Harriet bit into the orange and the juice streamed down her chin. Richard bent forward to mop her up with one of the white napkins, shaking his hand as he dabbed at juice stains on the fawn wool of the jersey she wore.

'You're ruining one of my favourite sweaters—I didn't realise you were such a messy eater or I'd have found a shabbier one for you to wear!'

Harriet sucked noisily on the orange before giving him

an unrepentant grin. 'I don't believe you own any shabby clothes. You must be one very successful farmer, that's all I can say. Where *is* this farm of yours, by the way?'

'Brazil,' he said casually, and took out one of the thin cigars he smoked, and lit it.

Harriet's eyes opened wide and she swallowed the last of the orange with a gulp. 'Brazil!'

'Yes. I'm the fifth generation of Liveseys to run the *fazenda*, or ranch, if you prefer. The main output is tobacco, but we have cattle and sheep, also. It's in the state of Rio Grande do Sul, near Port Alegre—or near as distances are measured in Brazil.' He tapped the ash from his cigar, his eyes absent on the valley below, and suddenly one or two things fell into place for Harriet.

'When I first saw you I thought you were a fisherman,' she said thoughtfully, 'not just because of the way you were dressed, but those fine white lines at the corners of your eyes give you the look of being accustomed to gazing out over long distances, plus the deep-dyed tan, of course. I suppose your *fazenda* is big, by British standards?'

'Yes.' He turned to look at her.

'What is it?' she asked, on the defensive at once.

'I was just thinking how different you look in Helio's old boots, with the rest of you bundled up in my sweater. No make-up, hair in a pigtail—not much like the elegant creature I rescued from the dance-floor of the Miramar.'

'This is me, just the same. One and the same person.' Harriet shrugged. 'Women are complex creatures in the main. During working hours I'm an efficient secretary, socially I'm a reasonably entertaining companion, I think, then there's the loving daughter, affectionate sister. A list very similar to any other unmarried woman of my age.' She turned to him suddenly, hugging her knees, her eyes intense and dark in her face, which had taken on a faint flush in the sunshine. 'But there is one person I most definitely am not, Richard, and that's the woman who was in your car with your young friend.'

Richard's eyes were sombre as they studied her face.

The brief moment of accord was gone and they sat looking at each other in silence broken only by the hum of insects and the rush of the river's progress far below.

'I wish I could believe that,' he said heavily at last, and ground his cigar out savagely with the heel of his boot. 'God knows part of me wants to—no, *does* believe it, but it's the part that governs my baser instincts, I'm afraid. My mind, my reasoning faculties, keep reminding me of the photograph in Penry's possession.'

All at once the day seemed dull. The sun still shone, but depression invaded Harriet's spirit like a fog, rendering everything a uniform grey. She turned away with a sigh and leaned her chin on her knees above her clasped hands. It was silly to feel so flattened by Richard's words, she reflected. To give him his due the man must have believed unshakably in her guilt, or he would hardly have gone to such lengths to get her here like this. But what he could never have prearranged in all his elaborate preparations was the subtle punishment he had unknowingly achieved for his victim, who was lacerated by feelings which had nothing to do with shock and fear, or even her distaste for the primitive conditions of her unusual prison. The real turn of the knife came from the fact that however brutal a revenge he had in mind she was in love with Richard Livesey, to her infinite regret. Harriet stared blindly at the vista before her, seeing nothing of it as she faced the unpalatable truth. What a ghastly mess! Why on earth couldn't she have chosen someone like Jeremy to fall in love with, or Simon Hadly, Guy's locum, or any one of several young men in the set she went out with in Leamington. Anyone at all, in fact, other than this large, intimidating man. She ground her teeth impotently. It was so unfair! Why should she be found guilty of a crime she had never committed all because Penry, whoever he was, was lying his socks off. A wave of hopelessness swept over her, and she shivered.

'Are you cold?' asked Richard courteously.

Harriet looked at him blankly and shook her head.

'Someone dancing on my grave.'

'Right, let's get moving, then—unless you're stiff and would prefer to turn back?'

From the look in his eyes she was fairly sure he expected her to say yes, and her head came up proudly. 'Of course not, I'd love to a ride a little further.'

She put her foot in Richard's hand and swung up on to Menina's back, patting the little horse affectionately as they set off again on their leisurely ride. It seemed best to pretend that the recent exchange of words had never occurred and Harriet asked polite questions about her surroundings and Richard answered in kind, avoiding personalities with equal care. After an hour or so he pronounced the ride long enough and they began the long upward return journey. Diablo had shown signs of friskiness during the morning, only Richard's firm hand keeping him to Menina's leisurely gait, but as the way back became gradually steeper even the chestnut's enthusiasm calmed down. As they climbed steadily Harriet's back began to ache badly from the unaccustomed exercise and she turned to questions about the vines to take her mind off it. At first she listened to Richard's answers with assumed attention, but very soon her interest was caught as he described the surprisingly primitive methods still employed in the small vineyard worked by the tenants of the Monteiro family.

'You mean they still actually *tread* the grapes here?' she asked in astonishment.

Richard nodded. 'The *vindima*—vintage—takes place at the end of September or beginning of October, at that mysterious moment when the sugar content of the grapes is pronounced right. It's a chancy business, very dependent on the weather—if it rains during the vintage the quality of the wine is considerably reduced.'

'How long does the actual vintage last?'

'From beginning to end about a month. Once picked the grapes must be trodden within two days, or almost immediately if it's very hot, which makes fermentation very rapid.'

Harriet gathered her reins in more tightly as Menina stumbled over a fallen branch, and patted the horse soothingly. Richard checked Diablo until Menina caught up. 'All right?' he asked.

Harriet saw no point in telling him about her back, and smiled brightly. 'Fine. Go on about the vineyard. Is there a big output?'

'Generally about seven thousand litres or so; not very large. It's done in four batches. They use big open granite vats set on bases and each vat must be cleaned and sterilised between batches.' He tilted his hat lower over his forehead and slanted a sardonic smile at her. 'Don't hit me again if I tell you that only men are allowed to tread the grapes, at which time the women keep right out of the way.'

'Why?' she asked rashly, and saw him catch his lower lip in his teeth.

'The process is reputed to—er—render them excessively virile,' he said, poker-faced.

Harriet laughed involuntarily. 'Personal experience, of course!'

'Of course.' He smiled, keeping his eyes on the path.

'What happens when the wine is truly trodden?'

'It's sucked through a rubber tube to see if it's ready, and if it is, the *flor*—flower—of the wine is run out and the pips and skins left. So off they go again and the latter are trodden by foot and the juice extracted. This is called the *pe*—the foot. The pulp left after this is put in a wooden press and the dark liquid extracted from it is mixed with the "flower" and the "foot" to arrive at the final wine which is stored in barrels—preferably oak casks.'

'Fascinating!' said Harriet. 'When do they bottle it?'

'That's all part of the mystique,' he told her. 'It must be some time towards the end of January on the day—preferably frosty—of the new moon.'

'Wow—how poetic! I'll never drink a glass of wine without remembering that in future.'

'Ah, but that's only the wine from this particular neck of the woods,' he reminded her. 'Automation and machinery have overtaken much of the industry elsewhere.'

Harriet sighed regretfully. 'Seems such a shame, somehow. Surely machinery doesn't produce the same flavour, or bouquet or whatever you call it as the process you just described?'

He chuckled. 'Spoken like a true romantic!'

She joined in, then caught her breath at the sharp twinge from her lumbar regions and bit her lip.

'I knew we'd gone too far,' said Richard sharply.

Much too far, thought Harriet bleakly. Her entire stay in Portugal was going to take a lot of getting over, one way and another. 'I'll survive,' she said through clenched teeth.

'I'll get Isabel to prepare a hot bath for you when we get back,' he said brusquely.

'Is there a bath?' she asked, diverted.

He nodded, grinning. 'I'll bring it into your room— only a hip-bath, I should warn you.'

Harriet didn't much care what it was as long as it was some kind of receptacle big enough to hold both her and a few gallons of hot water. By the time she crumpled into Richard's waiting arms outside the house at long last she was incapable of hiding the fact that she could hardly stand. Menina's plodding, easy gait had been very deceptive, deluding her into believing she could ride for hours without suffering any ill-effects, and now she was paying for it.

Isabel came scurrying from the kitchen, followed by a youth with black curly hair and a pleasant smile.

'Helio,' said Richard briefly as he took Harriet's weight against him.

Harriet smiled at the boy and pointed at her boots as Helio took charge of the horses. '*Obrigado*,' she gasped, and the boy flushed bright red with pleasure, saying something unintelligible to her in return as he led the horses away.'

'He said it was an honour,' Richard informed her, and gave a stream of instructions to the deeply concerned Isabel, and the old woman shuffled off rapidly to do his bidding.

Every moment was agony as Harriet staggered along the verandah, hanging on to Richard like grim death until he picked her up impatiently. 'It's easier to carry you than drag you,' he said, brushing aside her protests, and strode quickly to her room to deposit her on the bed.

'Give me your foot,' he ordered and she complied, wincing as he pulled off each boot in turn. 'A good thing they were loose,' he added, 'or the process could have been a lot more painful.'

Harriet found that hard to believe at that precise moment and lay on her back, gasping like a stranded fish as Richard left the room. He was back almost immediately with a hip-bath of the type Harriet had seen only in museums before. From then it was all go as Richard and Helio sprinted in and out with kettles and pans of hot water until there was enough in the bath to immerse her satisfactorily.

'Won't it be too hot?' she asked, eyeing the steam nervously.

'Not by the time you've taken your clothes off.' Richard's scrutiny swept from the sweater, which was loose, to the jeans, which were not. 'I'd offer to lend a hand if I thought you'd accept it, but as I'm sure you won't I'll send Isabel along to help.'

Harriet would have preferred to manage without any help at all, but common sense told her that while she might possibly manage to divest herself of sweater and shirt, the jeans were an insurmountable obstacle.

'Thank you,' she said faintly to Richard's retreating back, and tried her best to make a start once he was out of the room, but she had only got as far as removing the ultra-large sweater by the time Isabel came hurrying to assist, clucking with sympathy as she helped Harriet to remove the rest of her clothes with surprising efficiency. She touched Harriet's hair with shy admiration as she helped the girl into the steaming tub.

'*Que beleza,*' she said reverently, and tears of gratitude stung Harriet's eyes as she lay back in the water, which was so hot it took her breath away at first. Not that she cared much as the heat permeated through her body and her aching muscles began to relax, helped on considerably by the action of several handfuls of herbs Isabel threw in the water, which gave off an immediate aromatic scent, and Harriet closed her eyes in bliss.

'*Obrigado,*' she sighed gratefully, making a mental resolve to learn a few more words of Portuguese if only to let the old woman know how much her kindness was appreciated. Isabel gathered up Harriet's clothes and bore them out of the room, then returned a few minutes later staggering under the weight of a steaming kettle and an armful of clean towels.

'*Mais agua quente,*' she said firmly as she poured the hot water carefully into the tub, and Harriet gasped her thanks, wondering if she looked as hot as she felt. Perspiration poured down her face as she watched the old woman take the beautiful cover from the bed and fold it with care before laying it reverently over the chair. Then she stripped off the top blankets and sheet and spread a large white towel on the bed. She helped Harriet from the water and wrapped her in another towel, rubbing her briskly and motioning her to do the same herself. Finding she could now actually move again, Harriet joined in enthusiastically until every centimetre of skin on her body felt alive and tingling. Obeying Isabel's gestures, she lay face down on the bed, her head turned to watch Isabel pouring oil into her cupped palm before applying it to her aching back. The oil smelt of the same herbs Isabel had put in the bath, the perfume sweet and pungent as the oil met Harriet's heated skin, and the old woman's hard hands began to massage the afflicted muscles beneath it. By this time she took Isabel's skill for granted as the gnarled brown fingers moved over her with a magic touch that first pummelled, then soothed, unlocking the pain and releasing all the tension, returning the slender body to something like normal again instead of the bundle of aches and pains that had practically tumbled from Menina's pretty little back.

CHAPTER SIX

AFTER Isabel had completed her ministrations she took away the towels and brought the all-enveloping white nightgown to slide over Harriet's head, stacked the pillows behind her and replaced the covers, by which time Harriet felt as warm as toast and more comfortable than she would have thought remotely possible, half an hour or so earlier. Before leaving her alone Isabel placed her book in her hand and mimed her instructions to her patient on staying in the warm bed for a while. Harriet relaxed gratefully against the pillows, feeling rather a fraud to be lying in bed at this hour, but revelling in her physical well-being, and wondering idly about what shocks dinner might have for her later on. No doubt the menu had been planned in advance by Richard as part of the campaign devised for her benefit. She frowned suspiciously. Perhaps even the ride today had allowed for her aching back at the end of it as part of the punishment plan. It was amazing that a man could go to such lengths for the sake of someone else, particularly when her host was obliged to put up with exactly the same inconveniences as herself. Not that roughing it seemed to trouble him in the slightest, she thought acidly, then smiled as she realised that after that wonderful bath and massage she wasn't all that troubled by the lack of mod cons herself.

Harriet was beginning to find the light from the oil-lamp a little dim for reading by the time a knock sounded on the half-open door and Richard appeared, carrying two glasses.

'May I come in?' he asked.

'Of course.' She eyed him cautiously as he came to the side of the bed and handed her one of the glasses.

'Sherry,' he said.

'Thank you.' She sipped at the pale-gold wine, wondering what sort of mood Richard was in this evening, noting that he looked vastly different from her companion on horseback. His chin was closely shaven and he wore grey tweed trousers of impeccable cut with a white shirt and the blue cashmere jersey she remembered from the journey.

'Why the analytical look?' he enquired, and leaned indolently against the bedpost.

'You were wearing those clothes in the car.'

'The only other sweater I brought is stained with orange-juice,' he said, straight-faced, 'so my choice was limited—and I felt you might object to the sheepskin jerkin at the dinner-table.'

'Oh, I don't know. It has a certain homespun charm.' Harriet's tone was as dry as the fino in her glass.

'I came to ask if you were able to make it to that same dinner table, or do you want me to bring you a tray in here?'

'No! I'll get dressed in a moment. It was Isabel who insisted I get into bed, and I felt so wonderful after her miraculous soothing hands that I was only too happy to stay here until dinner-time.'

'Isabel's well known in these parts for her healing skills. She and Helio have gone by now, of course, but dinner's ready when you are.' The expression in Richard's blue eyes made Harriet uneasy as he made a leisurely inspection of her appearance. 'You look like something from another century with your hair hanging loose over that virginal nightgown—though the general effect is somewhat at odds with the message worked into the counterpane.'

She frowned at him and craned her head to read the words in the lace insertion of the linen cover. 'Why? What do they say?'

He leaned forward, resting one knee on the edge of the bed as he traced the pattern with fingers that lingered deliberately on the lace pulled taut across Harriet's midriff, and involuntarily her muscles contracted in response to the delicate pressure.

'Here we have the heart the Portuguese love to work into their embroidery.' Richard's finger paused. 'See? It's very slightly turned to one side. And here near by is the key, which represents the love to open it.' He smiled into her watchful, tense face. 'The words worked below are "*Boa noite, meu amor*". In other words "Good night, my love".'

'How charming,' said Harriet evenly.

He straightened and stood up. 'Can you manage to dress yourself?'

'Of course.' She downed the rest of the sherry and handed him the glass. 'Thank you, that was lovely. If you'll give me ten minutes I'll be ready.'

'Splendid,' he murmured, and strolled from the room, closing the door carefully behind him.

Harriet slid from the bed, much relieved to find herself mobile again. Her neck was still protesting a little, it was true, but compared to its condition when she dismounted from Menina it was surprisingly normal, and swiftly she put on fresh underwear and stockings, zipped up the blue linen skirt and added her white cotton sweater. Her shirt was being laundered, no doubt, but a string of coral beads found in her overnight bag softened the bare round neckline and the grey-suede slippers added a touch of elegance. She brushed her hair and gathered it up into a careless knot on top of her head, securing it with her own gilt pins and Isabel's tortoiseshell combs, and allowed a few curling tendrils to soften the effect at her ears and the nape of her neck, then stared into the mirror for a moment or two wondering whether to go the whole hog and gild the lily for her host's benefit. Her eyes narrowed, glittering darkly at her in the dim light from the oil-lamp. Richard might be working along the lines of crime and punishment, but she was fairly sure he was by no means immune to her, just the same. Some indefinable nuance in his manner towards her told her plainly enough that while he might dislike her, despise her even, he was very definitely not indifferent to her physical attributes, at least. She smiled at her reflection dreamily. It would be very, very satisfactory to turn the tables on him and make him actually succumb to her charms so that she could repulse him at the worst possible moment—or best, depending on which way one looked at it.

A few minutes later, her face made up with all the skill she could muster, Harriet walked along the verandah to the welcoming glow of the kitchen in a cloud of perfume, a new confidence in the assured tap of her slender heels on the worn old boards. Richard sprang to his feet as she went into the room, the sudden deadpan set of his face betraying his reaction to her as clearly as if he'd actually admitted it. The room was warm from the great log fire banked in the hearth, and as usual a savoury smell hung tantalisingly in the air.

'What am I to be tested with tonight?' Harriet smiled brilliantly at Richard as he drew out a chair for her and surprise showed fleetingly in his eyes, giving her a little glow of triumph. It would work, she felt sure, and accepted the glass of sherry he gave her.

'We were to have enjoyed one of Isabel's specialities: *miolos mexidos com ovos*,' he said, a smile lifting the corners of his mouth. 'Technically, alas, it proved impractical since it needs to be served as soon as it's prepared because of the scrambled eggs.'

'Scrambled eggs?' Harriet's eyes sparkled at him

mischievously. 'Oh, come on—surely you ordered something more alien than that to delight me!'

'The eggs are served with fried lambs' brains,' he admitted, grinning.

'Glory!' she shuddered. 'I think you would have beaten me there.' She gave a suspicious glance at the big pot suspended over the fire. 'I wonder what's in there? It smells marvellous, but then so did the famous pigs' trotters!'

'Isabel says it's quite filling, so I persuaded her that melon in port wine would make a good first course and leave you with plenty of enthusiasm for the *dobrado* to follow.'

'*Dobrado*?'

'*Dobrado a moda do Porto*, to give it its full title—tripe,' added Richard blandly.

'Tripe,' echoed Harriet faintly, then remembering her new resolution smiled at him with faint reproach in her wide dark eyes. 'You're a very unrelenting man, Richard Livesey!'

'Because I'm giving you tripe for dinner?'

'And in many other ways, too.' She sipped her sherry, her eyes holding his. 'When are you going to take me back?'

'In good time, you have my word.' His eyes were very steady. 'I never break it, I assure you.'

'Never?'

'No. Not even when keeping it sometimes wars with other instincts.' This time there was a flare of heat in the cold blue eyes, and Harriet rejoiced inwardly.

'Are you saying you don't relish the job of gaoler, Richard?'

'Shall we say I don't relish the necessity that prompted me to take on the role.' His face was sombre as he got up to refill their glasses.

'Is that why you're being such a forebearing captor?'

He looked up sharply. 'Forbearing?'

Harriet nodded, her eyes limpid with innocence. 'If

you were being wholeheartedly punitive wouldn't I be
housed in a less exotic bedroom—or at least confined to it
on bread and water? The drugged fruit juice and the
kidnap were splendidly *de rigueur*, but since then I rather
think I've been a little pampered compared to the
average hostage!'

For a moment she thought she'd gone too far as the
thunderous look on Richard's face made her quail
inwardly, then suddenly a grudging smile curved his
wide, expressive mouth.

'You're right, of course,' he admitted, surprising her
still more. 'I intended to frighten you out of your wits,
show you what it was like to wake up still feeling the
after-effects of drugs and not knowing where the hell you
were or how you got there.'

'Well, you succeeded there,' said Harriet drily. 'When
I woke up I thought I was off my head. That room doesn't
give much of a lift to the spirits, does it?' She regarded
him curiously. 'But since then you've allowed me to
explore the house, taken me for a ride, I've had a bath
and massage—in fact the worst part of my punishment
has been certain items of cuisine.'

'You make it difficult for me, Harriet.' His fingers
played with the battered silver cutlery laid out on the
table. 'At times I have tremendous problems in remembering you're the type of woman capable of treating
Penry the way you did.'

Harriet forced back the angry denial on the tip of her
tongue, staring hard at his slim, hard hands. 'I suppose,'
she said carefully, 'it never occurs to you that Penry
might be mistaken? That photograph was taken some
time ago.'

Richard leaned forward across the table, his face
suddenly shedding its rigid mask of self-control. 'Of
course it occurs to me. Goddammit, Harriet, I didn't
want to believe you were the one! But after seeing you in
the flesh I knew any man would only have to see that hair
and face just once to remember it only too well for—for a

very long time. You're one of a kind, Harriet Neil.'

Harriet's long lashes drooped deliberately to conceal her expression, and she let them lie in thick brown crescents against her cheeks for a moment before she raised her lids slowly and looked Richard directly in the eye. Instantly the anger in his cold blue eyes kindled into something very different, and ignited a little flame of response deep inside her. She caught her full lower lip with her teeth and sighed.

'Then as there seems to be nothing I can do to change your opinion of me, shall we have dinner?'

It was deeply satisfying to witness the way he quite visibly had to pull himself together as he went to collect their melon from the larder leading off the kitchen.

'Shouldn't I be doing that?' asked Harriet as he put the plates on the table.

'Since you could hardly walk an hour or so ago I'll relax my rule and wait on you—just for tonight,' he said lightly.

She raised her eyebrows and began to eat her port-drenched slice of ripe cantaloupe melon. 'In that case I shall enjoy my meal all the more!'

To her surprise she was right. The tripe, which was cooked with chicken and sausage with carrots and tomatoes, was unexpectedly delicious. She demolished her modest portion with indelicate speed and got up to help herself to more, to Richard's amusement.

'I was starving,' she said defensively, 'and I have a very healthy appetite, so food has to be pretty strange before I fail to eat it, I assure you.'

Richard refilled her wine-glass and surrendered his own plate when Harriet offered him a second helping. 'With me the food has a fair area to refuel, so I don't put on any excess weight, but if you eat this much all the time how do you stay in shape?'

'I'm not exactly skinny!'

'Very true.' Richard's eyes made a leisurely journey over her shape as she set a full plate in front of him.

'Skinny is the last word I'd think of in connection with you.'

She laughed, her eyes dancing as she sat down to polish off her second plateful of the *dobrado*. 'I'm not sure whether that's a compliment or not. Though to be honest I'm normally a bit rounder than I am now. I had flu a few weeks ago and lost my appetite for a bit—tragedy! Was I glad when it came back! I haven't put back all the pounds I lost, though I soon will if I keep on wolfing double portions of Isabel's cooking. If you intended the *dobrado* as part of my punishment you failed sadly, by the way.' She took their plates to the sink, and left them there on Richard's instructions.

'Isabel was very put out when she found you'd washed up last night, so leave them for her—please. You may consider yourself a prisoner, but as far as she's concerned you're an honoured guest.'

'And what am I as far as you're concerned?' asked Harriet quickly.

Richard was quiet for a moment. 'I find that hard to answer,' he said at last. 'I brought you here to make you own up to what you did to Penry, but I'm beginning to get the feeling you'd die rather than admit you were guilty.'

'I'd rather I wasn't faced with such an extreme alternative,' she said cuttingly, 'but otherwise you're dead right, Mr Livesey. If I *were* guilty I'd own up, but I'm not, so I won't. I'll see you in hell first.'

'If you're as innocent as you make out you're hardly *likely* to see me there, are you?'

'Very true. Is there any pudding?'

Richard threw back his head and laughed out loud for the first time since they'd left the Algarve. 'I know what your punishment should have been—starvation!'

'It's too late for that now,' said Harriet smugly. 'Isabel would never let me go hungry.'

He nodded ruefully in agreement. 'You're right. She thinks you're the original fairy off the Christmas tree—

and strongly disapproves of my keeping you here, I may add.'

'Does she now! Why?'

'It goes against the conventions. She suspects my intentions towards you.' There was mockery in the smile he gave her. 'In her book I should bring only a bride to sleep in the Monteiro *cama de matrimonio*; the bed in your room.' He returned to the larder and brought out a large oval dish. 'Here's your pudding—*arroz doce*. Rice pudding is the traditional dessert at wedding feasts here, so it's probably Isabel's way of giving a hint. She's already asked if you're my *noiva*.'

'Noiva?' queried Harriet uneasily.

'Betrothed, fiancée, whatever.' Richard gestured towards the large dish. 'Anyway, for God's sake eat some of it, if only to please Isabel.'

Harriet looked at the sign of the cross traced on the surface of the pudding in cinammon and helped herself to a small portion.

Richard smiled faintly. 'Perhaps she's trying to invest me with an odour of sanctity, though actually it's quite common to decorate sweets with the cross, or the ubiquitous heart.'

Harriet laid down her spoon after only a few mouthfuls, and leaned back in her chair with a sigh. 'Delicious, but very filling—*you* didn't have any, I notice.'

'I don't care for sweet things.' Richard poured the last of the wine into their glasses and lit a cigar. 'Shall I pull your chair over to the fire?'

'Yes, please.' It was a lot chillier in this part of the country than in the Algarve and Harriet wished she'd brought some warmer clothes with her, then laughed inwardly. This part of the holiday was a bit unexpected. She could hardly have been expected to provide for being kidnapped when she set out on her trip to Lisbon. Her mouth drooped a little as she stared into the glowing fire.

'Penny for your thoughts,' said Richard, glancing at

her face as he brought his chair near hers.

'Not worth it.' Harriet glanced about her curiously at the big, dimly lit room, conscious of the air of disuse and decay that hung in the air despite the big fire and the scents of cooking. 'No one actually lives here, do they?' she asked abruptly. 'This house hasn't been lived in for years, I'm sure.'

'No,' he admitted. 'The home of the Monteiros is in Viano do Castelo these days since their main income comes from ship-building. João Monteiro, the present head of the family, lives there; so do his younger brothers, all my generation. João's a marine engineer, Eduardo's the financial man, José is in the army, and their sisters are both married to engineers who work in the business.'

'Then this place belongs to João,' said Harriet.

'No, it belongs to all of them. Under Portuguese law all children have equal rights to inheritance, girls as well, so even the largest estates get divided and subdivided as time goes on. In this case the Monteiros have gone into industry elsewhere and the land in this area is leased to tenants who grow vines and work a few individual hectares of land.'

'And this house?'

'Kept as a museum, more or less. Nothing in the place is of much value.'

'But surely the furniture in my room is worth a great deal,' contradicted Harriet.

He gave her an odd smile. 'I borrowed it from the Monteiros in Viano do Castelo just for the occasion.'

'What a lot of trouble you've taken,' said Harriet wonderingly, then frowned. 'Doesn't anyone èver try to break in?'

Richard shook his head. 'Too remote for strangers, and apart from Isabel and Helio, who act as caretakers and tidy the place up a bit, no one local would touch the place with a barge-pole anyway.'

Harriet felt suddenly cold. 'Why?' she demanded.

'It's reputed to be haunted.'

She let out an explosive breath. 'Great! That's all I needed—ghosts for company. Now you're really doing well!'

He laughed mockingly. 'Oh, come on, Harriet, don't tell me a modern girl like you believes in ghosts!'

'If you'd asked me that in the Miramar, or even back in my flat in Leamington, I'd have laughed at you.' She waved a hand at the room resentfully. 'But here, with only lamplight and shadows, not to mention the general aura of crumbling decay, I'm not so sure. Apart from this kitchen it's so cold in the house, too. That room of mine is like a tomb ...' She stopped as she saw Richard's expression. 'What is it?' she asked apprehensively.

'That's the actual part of the house supposed to be haunted,' he said apologetically.

Harriet slumped in her chair. 'Congratulations on your success! Forget about the drugs, the weird food, the lack of mod cons. All you ever needed as my punishment was a ghost for bedfellow, and I confess it freely.'

'But it's all nonsense, Harriet,' he retorted.

She glared at him. 'That's all very well here in the light by the fire, but back there in that huge bed in the dark I know I'm going to find it hard to convince myself of it, just the same.'

Richard got up and brought coffee-cups from the table, filling them from the pot beside the fire. 'Here, drink this and then have some brandy.'

'The coffee's fine, but no brandy, thanks. I've had more than enough to drink already.'

'But you're shivering, woman!'

'From fright, not cold!'

Richard thrust a glass into her cold fingers. 'Don't be childish, Harriet. Drink this cognac and you'll feel better.'

Harriet did as he said mutinously, swallowing the fiery spirit in one great gulp like a dose of medicine. Warmth spread through her instantly, but she still felt dread at the thought of returning to her bedroom. The fact that she was behaving irrationally was no help to her. She knew she was being silly, but somehow Richard's information only confirmed the feeling she had experienced from the beginning in that gloomy chamber.

'Tell me the worst,' she said, resigned. 'If there is a ghost I'd rather know who he is.'

'She, actually.' He shot a frowning glance at her. 'I don't know that it's a good thing to give you the details—rather like putting ideas in your head.'

'For God's sake just tell me,' she snapped. 'It's preferable to making up a hundred grisly theories of my own.'

He looked doubtful, and replenished the fire with more logs before he began to talk. The story he had to tell was all the more poignant and frightening to Harriet as she listened, because it had happened only a couple of generations before, rather than in the dim and distant past. Richard had been given the details by his grandmother, who had been in the house when the tragedy happened, infusing the story with a vivid immediacy most ghost stories lacked.

Francisco Monteiro had been the only son of a country squire who sent him to the Jesuit boarding school in Braga for his education. There he became acquainted with the Cardoso brothers, who befriended the homesick young man from the country and took him home occasionally to their sophisticated town home in Braga to meet their parents and their young, very beautiful sister Sofia. The Cardosos were aristocracy, once attached to the court, and had only retired to provincial Braga when the monarchy was expelled to Brazil to escape Napoleon. But by this time, many years later, the Cardosos were no longer wealthy, unlike the Monteiros, and when the young Francisco became enamoured of Sofia she was betrothed to the young man from the country with alacrity by her practical parents.

During the engagement, went on Richard, the pair

saw each other infrequently, because the journey from the Monteiro estates to Braga was long and arduous, and necessitated two changes of horses in those days. So, when Francisco finally bore his bride home in triumph the young pair were still virtually strangers, with love and desire on one side and shrinking reluctance on the other. The bridal chamber had been prepared with care for Sofia, with a hand-carved rosewood bed from Goa in pride of place where, at the appointed hour, the girl had lain shivering under the embroidered cover, wearing a voluminous nightgown that covered every inch of her except her white, terrified face as her young husband, flushed with the wine pressed on him by the male guests, burst into the room to claim his long-awaited prize.

One of the logs on the fire gave a loud crack and Harriet jumped almost out of her skin. 'What happened then?' she asked urgently.

'My grandmother always grew euphemistic and vague at this point,' said Richard drily. 'I gather there was quite a struggle when—when Francisco tried to consummate the marriage. There were terrible screams, then silence, except for the agonised sobs of the unfortunate bride-groom. When his father ran into the room the girl was dead, her skull broken against the heavy carving of the headboard.'

'My God!' Harriet swallowed hard and hardly noticed when Richard poured more brandy into her glass. She drank it absently, her eyes huge as she stared at his face. 'What happened to poor Francisco? Did he mourn for her and shut the bedroom up?'

Richard suddenly dazzled her with the brilliant, lopsided smile she had never expected to see again. 'Not a bit of it,' he said cheerfully. 'Soon afterwards he married a local lady who was far more co-operative, and presented him with six children in double quick time, all born in the same bed. My grandmother, who had been in the house on that fateful wedding night, was despatched on holiday to relatives in Brazil to get over the shock (where she met and married my grandfather, incidentally), and the Monteiro parents went off to live in Viana do Castelo. Francisco, I'm told, tried to forget that Sofia ever existed and would never have her name spoken in the house. But people have sworn that on certain nights you can still hear her screaming. Which, of course, is utter rot,' he concluded briskly.

Harriet leaned her head in her hand and stared into the fire. 'Of course it is,' she agreed, without conviction.

'You don't believe in all that rubbish?' asked Richard mockingly.

'You must have thought I would or you wouldn't have told me about it.' She got up quickly and stood glaring at him. 'Well, I hope revenge is sweet, Richard Livesey. I'm scared of my own shadow after that grisly little tale—which no doubt was the object of the exercise!'

He laughed softly and stood up, catching hold of her elbow as she swayed a little. 'You're very slightly tight, you know, Harriet.'

She pulled away with dignity. 'I am not.' She cast her mind over her alcohol consumption during the evening and frowned. After sherry, wine and brandy in quick succession he could be right, of course. Then she remembered something else. She had fully intended flirting with Richard until he couldn't resist making love to her, now she thought of it. With a quick change of tactics she smiled at him tentatively, her eyes dark and inviting in her fire-flushed face. 'Will you walk back with me?' she asked. 'And could I have another lamp?'

'Why go to bed at all yet?' he countered. 'It's not late. Are you tired?'

'No.' Harriet hesitated. 'I just thought I'd get it over with. The longer I leave it the less I'll fancy going back to that room.'

'Then stay a little longer.'

'Would you like me to?' This was better, she thought. He was picking up his cue beautifully.

'I would, very much.' He smiled again, and she

blinked. 'What is it? he asked quietly, and took her hand.

Harriet moved a little closer. 'You're being nice to me. Why?'

'I think you know why.' He took her hand up to his cheek and held it there for a second, holding her eyes with his, his breathing beginning to quicken. 'I want very badly to kiss you again, Harriet.'

'Even though I'm such a sinner?' she breathed artlessly.

'Perhaps I can reform you,' he murmured, and dropped her hand to pull her close against him.

Harriet leaned against him pliantly, her eyes closing to hide the triumph in them. How easy it had been. She surrendered her mouth and slid her arms round his neck, wondering how far she should let him go, how much she should let him suffer before she shut the door in his face. Richard sat down in the chair, taking her with him without moving his mouth from hers. He kissed her with a fire that made her gasp, while his hand caught the fullness of her breast. Harriet wriggled in his lap and he groaned, one arm tightening cruelly around her while his other hand moved beneath her sweater, seeking her nipple through its gossamer-thin covering as his kisses grew fierce with a demand that made her dizzy, sapped her will, kept her from thinking. Harriet moaned and slid further down in his embrace until she suddenly remembered that all this was to send *Richard* mad, not her. She began to struggle, but the man curved over her mistook the struggles for enthusiasm, and he raised his head a little to look at her flushed face with eyes that looked black, red gleams from the fire reflected in their depths as he slid one long-fingered hand up her thigh and found the warm, smooth skin above her stocking.

Harriet began to struggle in earnest, but Richard's breathless laugh was indulgent as his mouth crushed hers again, silencing her protests and subduing her as she tried to push his hand away. What a fool you are! her mind screamed silently as she twisted violently in his arms, then he caught both her hands in his, his mouth closed over hers, and his questing fingers slid up her thigh to find the hot, secret target they were seeking. Harriet went berserk, arching in his grasp until her spine threatened to crack and then somehow she was free and on her feet and running without a thought for ghosts or spiders or anything else but sanctuary in her bedroom, where the ghost of a long-dead girl held fewer terrors than the living presence of Richard Livesey.

The oil-lamp in the bedroom was still alight and she muttered a prayer of thanks as she heaved the washstand across the door, and threw off her clothes, tearing the combs and pins from her hair once she was in her nightgown, her own, normal nightgown, not the shroud-like garment she strongly suspected had once belonged to the doomed Sofia. Half sobbing with emotion and anger, she crawled under the covers and pulled them over her head, huddling in the middle of the bed like a frightened child.

Her smug little plan had gone horribly wrong. She should have stopped Richard sooner and left with dignity. Instead of which it had been a frantic effort to stop at all. It was *she* who had fallen into the trap, her whole body on fire and clamouring for him to go on, to complete what he had started. Her hands twisted in her hair as she burrowed into the pillows, her face burning with shame. What an idiot she was to love a man, want him to make love to her so violently she felt sick with frustration from the feelings kindled in her body, when all the time he thought she was some drug-pushing little tramp. Worn out with self-loathing and the rigours of the long day, Harriet eventually went to sleep once she had stopped listening for the rattle of the doorhandle and the sound of Richard's voice. It was dark in the room when she woke. The lamp was out and ghostly moonlight filtered through the room, and Harriet put a hand to her throat in horror, her blood running cold as screaming sounded through the room, faint at first, rising to a terrible climax, and she sat rigid in the bed, eyes tightly shut in terror and her hands clamped over her ears until the shock of shattering glass pierced her frenzy and Richard's voice was shouting 'Harriet, Harriet!' and the screaming stopped and there was only her own sobbing.

'For God's sake, Harriet!' Richard sat on the edge of the bed and hauled her into his arms, holding her close against his bare chest and stroking her hair, gentling her into silence. Harriet drew back, gasping, and looked down at herself, at her nightgown which was bias cut and clinging, and apricot satin instead of hand-woven linen.

'You're all right now, Harriet, you were dreaming,' said Richard soothingly in the darkness, and drew her back into his arms.

'But the nightgown——' she said huskily. 'I was wearing the other one—Sofia's nightgown with the lace, and she was screaming——'

His arms tightened and he laid his cheek on her hair. 'You were having a nightmare, sweetheart. *You* were screaming, and I had to break the window to get in because you'd barricaded the door. It's all my fault——'

'You mean I dreamt I was wearing Sofia's nightgown?' said Harriet incredulously.

He ran a hand down her back. 'You certainly did. What I can feel is satin, surely, and in any case the other one isn't Sofia's, it's Isabel's. So is the counterpane.'

'Oh.' Harriet suddenly felt very silly, and drew away, glad she couldn't see his face plainly. 'I'm so sorry I woke you.'

'I wasn't asleep.' His voice sounded grim. 'And I'm the one who should apologise. The story I told you was fabrication.'

'*What*? You mean the room isn't haunted? There's no Sofia?'

'There was a Sofia all right. She was my great-aunt and everything else is true about the story apart from the wedding night. As far as anyone knows that proceeded along pretty much the same lines as anyone else's. *She* was the one who presented Francisco with six children.'

Harriet scrambled back under the bedclothes, speechless with rage. Richard stood up, his silhouette black against the faint light from the window. 'Aren't you going to say anything?' he asked.

'Only that you can go back to wherever you came from now you've had your little joke, achieved your object. It must be madly amusing to scare someone to death—I must try it some time!' Her voice quavered a little, the tears still very near the surface.

'I'm deeply sorry, Harriet.' The deep voice certainly sounded remorseful in the darkness. 'If it's any consolation I could kick myself for frightening you so badly.'

'Just one thing before you go,' she said conversationally. 'Will you tell me why? Was it because I took all the rest of it too much in my stride? Or was it because I wouldn't own up to being this mysterious criminal of yours?'

'You won't like the truth.' Richard came nearer, standing at the edge of the bed. 'But since truth is what we're dealing in at the moment I suppose I'd better confess that I had some crack-brained idea that if I managed to make you nervous enough you just might—and I stress the doubt factor—well, that you might agree to my company in your bed as protection against things that go bump in the night.'

Harriet's jaw dropped and she closed her mouth with a snap. 'You did all that just to insinuate yourself into my bed where, in your opinion, so many men have gone before?'

'Yes. Tonight—earlier on—I didn't care how many men you'd had as long as here and now you wanted *me*. I could have sworn you felt the same, Harriet. I'm not a schoolboy, I know——' He stopped short as he heard her intake of breath, then he sat on the bed beside her and groped for her hand in the darkness. 'I didn't mean that the way you think. I wasn't thinking about Penry. God help me, I haven't given him a thought all night. I meant

I'm old enough to know when a woman is genuinely responsive. What I don't understand is why you started to fight me like a tigress.'

Harriet tried to snatch her hand away, but he wouldn't let it go. 'I would have thought it was obvious,' she said bitterly. 'How could I let you make love to me when I know exactly what kind of woman you think I am?'

Richard moved closer. 'I'm past caring what kind of woman you are,' he said unsteadily. 'All I know is that I want you more than I've ever wanted anyone or anything in my life before. I'm being honest, Harriet. From the moment I first laid eyes on you I've wanted to make love to you until neither you nor I care a damn who we are beyond the fact that we're a man and a woman who need each other.'

'So why have you been so cold and overbearing?' she cried. 'Why won't you *believe* me?'

He grasped her shoulders and pulled her to him. 'You know why,' he said into her hair. 'God knows it should be easy enough to lie if that's the only way you'll give yourself to me, but I can't. But now I'm not thinking about Penry, or anyone else. I give up.'

With a swift movement he pulled the pillows away, and Harriet fell flat on her back with a cry of surprise he cut off with his mouth as he followed her down, holding her fast with her hair imprisoned under his body as he lay half on top of her. She tore her mouth away, gasping, and tried to free herself, but he captured her one free hand and held it to his lips, kissing it with a tenderness that breached her defences.

'Don't fight me any more, Harriet,' he breathed, and kissed her parted lips with a gentleness that sent a quiver through her body and his mouth grew fierce as hers responded tentatively. His hands began to move over her skin delicately, almost soothing in their seductive, slow insistence as he stroked her shoulders and back. He lifted himself away and she heard a slight rustle, then his naked body was close against hers as his mouth caressed her

face and wandered over her cheekbones and chin, sliding
down the curve of her throat to linger where a pulse
throbbed against his lips. Harriet lay perfectly still,
vanquished by the sheer pleasure of his touch, wanting
this subtle assault on her senses to go on and on. The
room held no terrors for her now. It seemed the fitting
setting for the discovery of love in Richard's arms, and
she moved her hands in his thick dark hair, about to tell
him, when he slid the satin straps from her shoulders and
moved his lips to her breasts. She forgot everything in the
white-hot streaks of sensation his mouth sent through her
trembling body. She wondered wildly why she was
shaking so much as he slid the nightgown from her body,
his breath rasping in his chest as he wound his hands in
her hair and lay half over her, with one hard thigh
thrown across her trembling legs.

'Don't be afraid,' he muttered hoarsely against her
mouth. 'Gently, gently . . .' and he trailed his hands over
her breasts to follow the curve of her waist, sliding under
her buttocks to lift her body up to him. She gave a choked
cry as his fingers sought the hidden place that throbbed
for him, and gasped, her head twisting from side to side
as he played havoc with her body in a way it had never
known before. He brought his mouth down hard on hers
at the exact moment he raised her hips to replace his
fingers with the hard thrust of his body. There was a
fleeting moment of semi-agony, then her body yielded
abruptly, arching against him in a mindless, basic need.
For a time she *had* no mind. There was only instinct, an
urge that grew more exacting, more imperative, impell-
ing her to some goal that would release the terrible,
beautiful tension threatening to tear her apart. But she
never reached it. Richard gave a gasp that seemed torn
from him, his body shuddered under her pummelling
hands and he lay still, leaving her stranded halfway to
some unknown destination.

Scalding tears welled from her eyes as she turned her
head aside, one hand brushing away Richard's hair from

her mouth as he lay against her breast. He moved, raising his head.

'I'm sorry,' he whispered, 'I'm so sorry, Harriet—I lost my head, to put it politely. I meant to take my time, but you were too much for me, too tempting——' A great tremor ran through his body and he moved up to pull her against him, stroking her tangled hair as he kissed her cheek. 'Tears?' he questioned.

Harriet had no way of describing the feeling that still held her taut as a violin-string against Richard's body. 'I don't know why,' she mumbled distinctly, and hid her face against his throat. He moved away a little and rescued the pillows, stacking them behind him before he drew her back into his arms.

'Shall I tell you what you won't tell me?' he asked softly.

She shrugged silently.

'I'm surprised you're not storming at me for being such a precipitate lover—the kind that puts his own pleasure first.' He kissed the tip of her nose. 'Let me light the lamp,' he said. 'I want to see you.'

'No!' said Harriet in desperation. She didn't want him to see her the way she was now, with her hair in a tangled mess and her eyes red.

'Then if you won't let me see you I must content myself with touch!' There was amusement in his deep voice as he pulled her up to sit in his lap. Harriet gave a little indignant sound of protest he silenced at once with his mouth as he held her still in the crook of his arm while his free hand began to stroke her breasts, moving from one to the other, pulling gently at her nipples and rolling them between his fingertips in a way that made her writhe against him as her lips parted beneath his. Almost at once she felt a stirring beneath her thighs and her eyes opened wide in the darkness.

'Richard——'

His answer was to thrust the covers away and lay her flat across the width of the bed. He parted her legs to find

her innermost secret place with his long fingers, and
kissed the smooth curve of her stomach as a low cry burst
from her throat and Harriet almost whimpered 'please,
please,' but the thrusting caress went on and on, driving
her wild as she twisted in an agony of pleasure. Then the
torment stopped and he was gone, and she scrambled to
her knees, suddenly motionless as she knelt there in the
soft light that filled the room. Richard bent to adjust the
lamp and turned to her, and her mouth dried. He stood
where he was for an instant, utterly still at the sight of
her, at her cascade of tangled hair spilling like gold over
her shoulders in the soft yellow light, and her eyes wide
and almost black in her flushed face. Harriet stared back,
mesmerised, unable to look away from the powerful male
figure. The skin on his body was paler than his forearms
and face, and his black hair was tousled wildly above
eyes that glittered with a look akin to disbelief as he stood
frozen for an instant before setting one knee on the bed
and dragging her up hard against his aroused body.

'Harriet,' he breathed against her mouth. 'You're
enough to drive a man mad!'

Harriet stared into his eyes, her desire for him so
overpowering it almost angered her that any man could
make her feel this way.

'What are you thinking?' he demanded.

'I'm *not* thinking,' she said flatly. 'All I seem able to do
is feel.'

A low, animal sound came from deep in Richard's
throat, and they fell together on the bed, twisting in a
tangle of limbs as each tried to get closer and closer to the
other. They were both breathing in short, agonised gasps
as Harriet's hands began an exploration of their own,
moving over his neck and shoulders and sliding down his
spine. She exulted as his muscles tensed at her touch and
grew bolder, moving lower, then paused as she stared
into his taut, clenched face, fiercely glad of the effect she
could see she was having on him.

'Don't stop,' he said raggedly, and seized her hand,

guiding it to the place she hadn't dared to touch. Every last shred of self-control deserted him abruptly as her fingers closed on him, and he tossed her on her back, parting her thighs to thrust himself deep within her throbbing body. For a moment they were both still, then Harriet's nails dug into the skin of his back and the storm broke. This time it was different, Harriet's senses keyed to such a pitch it was only moments before the agonising tension burst into a million throbbing fragments as she reached the unknown destination and found what waited for her there. Only seconds later the man above her reached the same glorious culmination, holding her cruelly tight as he gasped his pleasure against her breasts, and still coiled together, they fell asleep in each other's arms in the middle of the great *cama de matrimonio* which had sheltered so many other love-exhausted couples before them.

Harriet was alone when she woke, lying against ordered pillows with the covers pulled decorously up to her chin, and the room was dim in the first rays of light from the dawn. The lamp was out, and for a moment she lay wondering if it had all been a dream, then she realised she was naked beneath the covers and her face grew hot and her eyes dreamy as she remembered Richard's lovemaking. She lay watching the light grow brighter, then tensed at the sound of voices, her breath quickening at the thought of seeing him again. She stretched luxuriously, her mouth curved in a secret, reminiscent smile, then someone knocked at the door and she pushed frantically at her hair.

'Come in,' she called with anticipation, the smile on her face fading a little when she saw Isabel shuffling in. The old woman had her laundered clothes over one arm and carried a broom and shovel in the other hand. She laid the clothes on the chair and waved towards the shattered window, indicating that she was about to clear up the broken glass. Harriet smiled and thanked her, wondering how Richard had explained the accident, and after Isabel had departed jumped out of bed to wash herself all over with cold water from the pitcher on the washstand. The early morning air was chilly, nevertheless Harriet's cheeks burned as she found bruises in places impossible to explain away as anything but the attentions of a lover. Remembering the wild coming together in the night, she was sure Richard must have a few similar bruises this morning too, and smiled a catlike little smile of satisfaction at the thought.

She hurried into her clothes and brushed her hair with vigour, braiding it carelessly into a loose rope as she wondered whether they would go riding again, or if Richard would take her for a walk. She gazed into the mirror with dreaming eyes, aware that she didn't really mind what they did as long as they did it together, and smiled at her reflection, barely able to recognise the radiant creature in the mirror as the same girl who had woken up in this same room for the first time feeling ill and disorientated and bitterly disillusioned.

Harriet turned from the mirror quickly as she heard the last sound she expected to hear. A car was approaching the house, and she ran out on to the verandah, taken aback as the Mercedes glided to a halt on the hard-packed earth and Richard got out, dressed for the civilised world. He stood looking up at her, his face shuttered and withdrawn, and his blue eyes as cold and hard as though the events of the night had never been. Harriet's glad smile of greeting died, and a sick, cold feeling rose inside her like fog as she stared at him in silent shock.

'Good morning,' Richard said brusquely. 'I aplogise for sending Isabel to disturb you, but we need to make an early start.'

'You're taking me away from here?' She drew in a deep breath. 'Am I allowed to know my destination this time?'

'Of course. I'm taking you back to Praia do Ceu. That's what you so passionately wanted, I believe?'

For a long, charged moment their eyes locked together, then Harriet's dropped before the inimical look in Richard's.

'Yes,' she agreed quietly. 'Yes, it was.'

CHAPTER SEVEN

SHORTLY afterwards they were on their way. Harriet had begged a few minutes to pack and change her jeans for the blue skirt, and was about to strip the bed when Isabel hurried in with a cup of coffee, making scolding noises when she saw what Harriet was doing. The old woman stripped the covers from the bed, stopping short as she caught sight of the bloodstains on the sheet, her wise old eyes soft with understanding as they met the embarassment and dismay in Harriet's. She patted Harriet's arm, doing her best to demonstrate her sympathy, and Harriet tried to smile, pointing at the white nightdress which hung over the foot of the bed.

'*Obrigado*, Isabel.' She touched the woman's arm gently. 'Yours?'

Isabel nodded proudly, and Harriet turned away to search her hastily packed case for something to give the old woman as a gift, finally finding a scarf pin made from a gold coin. She held it out to Isabel and said '*obrigado*' repeatedly, and the old woman clutched it in delight, clasping her hands in gratitude.

Minutes later Harriet was seated in the car beside Richard as the Mercedes began the journey down the rough road they had ridden on horseback only the day before.

'Try to rest as much as possible,' he instructed tersely. 'We have a long ride ahead of us.' He glanced at her expressionlessly. 'I trust you're not too stiff today.'

Harriet's cheeks flamed, then cooled again as she

realised he was merely referring to her exertions on horseback. 'Not in the least. Thanks to Isabel I've no ill-effects at all.'

'Good.'

And that was that. There was no more communication between them. Harriet sat in utter misery, oblivious to the bumpiness of the journey down the track, unaware even of the smoother progress on the paved road when they reached it. She stared, dry-eyed, at the passing scenery, no more conscious of what she was seeing than she had been in the drugged sleep of the previous journey, her mind reeling in the effort to imagine what in heaven's name could have happened to transform last night's passionate lover into the silent, hostile man beside her. She forced back a sob, desperate to keep her grief hidden from him, pride holding her rigid in her seat and smothering the questions that rose in her throat to choke her. She stole only one glance at Richard's grim profile, then turned her eyes blindly ahead and kept them there, eventually forcing herself to blunt the edge of her searing hurt by sheer concentration on the beauty of the countryside as they drove through it.

Richard stopped in Braga, but only long enough to top up the car with petrol. Under normal circumstances Harriet would have liked to look round the town, particularly the Romanesque cathedral, and even in her present mood felt faint surprise at the number of churches everywhere, standing shoulder to shoulder with convents and handsome Renaissance houses. She wondered bleakly if one of the latter had once been the home of the famous Sofia Cardoso, but kept her speculation to herself, even though she couldn't resist a comment on Braga's superabundance of piety.

Richard nodded. 'The Portuguese have a saying: Coimbra sings, Porto works, Lisbon plays and Braga prays. Most people come here to visit the shrine of Bom Jesus,' he added, to her surprise. 'It stands on a hill outside the town, and there's a great stairway which folds in and out like a fan.'

Considerably taken aback by the unexpected burst of information, Harriet was none the less unsurprised when it apparently exhausted Richard's stock of conversation and silence reigned again as they headed south. She tried hard to doze as he had advised her, but it was impossible while questions buzzed about in her brain like angry bees, stinging away at the raw hurt his behaviour had dealt her.

The journey took them on past Oporto, and eventually they reached Coimbra, the ancient walled university town, where Richard stopped for lunch in a cafeteria-type restaurant on the quay. Harriet was desperate for the break by this time, but had no appetite for the food Richard insisted on ordering. She picked listlessly at unwanted sandwiches, but took care to drink the coffee he brought her, and the bottle of mineral water, remembering the thirst of the former trip.

'I feel that some explanation is due to you,' Richard said abruptly to her horror, as they finished the sketchy meal. Harriet's heart gave a sick thump.

'Quite unnecessary,' she said, and kept her eyes on her plate.

'Nevertheless I wanted to say that last night——'

'Forget about last night,' she cut in scornfully, and looked him straight in the eye. 'I assume you want to make it clear that as far as you're concerned I'm still the same criminal as before despite your moment of sexual aberration, and that I mustn't delude myself that it makes any difference. Have no fear. We'll pretend it never happened.' Her mouth curved in a cruel little smile. 'After all, it was nothing very momentous, was it?'

Richard's mouth tightened into a straight line, and he pushed his plate away, leaving most of the food uneaten. 'I'm glad you're able to dismiss it all so lightly.'

'Is there any reason why I shouldn't?' Harriet's eyes held a challenge and she exulted inwardly as his slid away. 'Actually I'm very pleased you're taking me back—at last. Now I shall be able to enjoy what's left of my holiday.' It gave her immense satisfaction to note the way he inhaled jerkily on the cigar he lit without remembering to ask her permission. 'Do smoke,' she added kindly, and was rewarded by the slight flush along Richard's high cheekbones.

'I'm sorry,' he said tightly. 'If you're ready we'll go.'

Harriet made a point of visiting the cloakroom and lingered there as long as she dared, splashing her face with cold water to try to calm herself down. So Mr Livesey had wanted to explain, had he? She looked at her pale face and laughed mirthlessly. Who knew what his explanation might have been? Nothing she could have borne to hear, judging by his previous comments. Probably his rejection meant she had been tried in some sexual balance and found wanting—it was obvious that only her physical attributes had any attraction for him, and she had no doubt been too inept, too amateur— Harriet gave a wild little sob. But amateur really meant being fond of something, didn't it; cultivating a pastime as an amusement? It therefore seemed pretty obvious that as far as Richard Livesey was concerned she had no talent to amuse as a lover. She wanted to plead with him, ask him what was wrong, every instinct screamed out to know what was the matter even while she shied violently away from the answer he might give.

Richard looked visibly strained by the time she steeled herself to rejoin him, and hurried her back to the car without ceremony.

'By the way,' said Harriet breathlessly, as he thrust her into the passenger seat, 'when do I get my money and passport?'

'When I deliver you at the hotel, and not before.' He ground out the cigar, looking at her levelly. 'I'm not that much of a fool.'

Which was the last thing he said until they stopped for a meal again after Lisbon, when he was constrained to consult her on her choice of food. Harriet almost choked on her grilled fish when it arrived, glad when they were on the road again, but not for long as her stomach, affected by the tension, chose to misbehave at intervals, and she had to implore Richard to stop the car on three separate occasions to allow her to be sick, which was the final straw. After the last mortifying episode she finally fell asleep for the last lap of the journey, and woke only when the car began bumping over an uneven bit of road. It was dark, and she had a splitting headache which worsened the moment she realised they were driving up a steep cobbled driveway to a house lit by several lamps in the garden surrounding it. She could just make out white walls, and the fact that the house was built on several levels adjoining a circular tower with a pointed roof, and that wherever it was, it certainly was not the Hotel Miramar.

'Where is this?' she asked coldly, as Richard brought the car to a halt into a courtyard.

'Torre Branca in Vale do Centianes,' he answered wearily.

'Where you've been staying?'

'Yes. Due to your—er—indisposition on the journey it's too late to take you directly to Praia do Ceu, so you'll sleep here for the night.'

'Is there any point in my objecting to the arrangement?'

'None whatsoever.' Richard sounded impatient. 'I'm too bloody tired to argue, so come in the house and try to be as quiet as you can. I don't want to wake anyone.'

Harriet was too tired to care if she did as she stumbled after him, and watched dully as he unlocked a door and motioned her before him into a hall with stark white walls. He opened a door on one side and ushered her into a room which would have delighted her at any other time. As Richard snapped on the bedside lamp she could see circular walls and a domed ceiling with a ceramic frieze she couldn't quite make out in the dim light. In any case her attention was taken up by the bed, which curved to follow the shape of the wall, and had a headboard carved to resemble a great shell. The thick white cotton spread covering it was plain, she noted with a wry twist of her mouth; no lace inserts or words of love this time. She stood mute, her eyes sombre as she stared at the bed, which reigned supreme in the room with only bedside tables and a carved wood chest to detract from its impact.

Richard gestured to another door. 'Bathroom through there. I'll see you in the morning.' And without a good night, or even a look at her, he left her alone.

Harriet looked at the closed door, then shrugged, and went to investigate the bathroom, which was the epitome of luxury after the old Monteiro house. The lure of the ivory sunken bath was irresistible and she ran wonderful hot water from gold taps shaped like shells and lay soaking for a while before drying herself on one of the fluffy ivory towels and stretching herself wearily on the bed. It seemed like mere seconds later that she was shocked awake by a hard hand on her shoulder and Richard's cold, insistent voice in her ear. She struggled to sit up, pushing her hair from her heavy eyes as she peered first at him, then her watch.

'It's not seven yet,' she said, yawning. 'It was hardly worth going to bed.'

Early as it was Richard was already shaved and showered, his hair curling damply above his temples. He wore a white fleece-lined sweatshirt and dark blue canvas trousers, and his face looked tired and austere.

'I thought you would like time for a bath before the introductions I'm forced to make,' he said distantly.

Harriet glared at him. 'I'm surprised you find introductions necessary at all. Can't we just sneak away without anyone even sullying their eyes with the sight of me?'

'No,' he snapped, 'we can't. I'll give you ten minutes to get yourself together, then I'll come back. Be ready.'

Harriet lay down again as he went out and shut her

eyes, feeling angry and hopeless. The night in the Monteiro marriage bed seemed like a fantasy, something that had never really happened. She clenched her fists under the covers and vowed bitterly to forget it ever had, to forget Richard's very existence once she was back home and everything was back to normal—whatever that was. She gave a mirthless little chuckle and opened her eyes, then gasped as she took in the details of the ceramic circling the ceiling above her head.

'Glory!' she exclaimed in awe. The theme of the beautiful frieze was the four seasons, executed with consummate artistry, and not a little eroticism, with nymphs and shepherds pursuing, and sometimes capturing, each other against a changing seasonal backcloth. Harriet's eyes almost started out of her head as she saw how some of the couples were occupied, and she scrambled out of bed in a hurry to cool her hot cheeks at the window, which was set deep in an embrasure in the wall.

The room she was in was at the top of the tower, and the rest of the house appeared to descend the hillside in tiers, each with a flagged terrace, the bottom one inlaid with a swimming-pool. The view was of undulating hills with houses scattered sporadically, but no sign of the sea. It was an enchanted landscape just the same, thought Harriet wistfully as she gazed down on the flower-filled garden, which was shady with what she thought must be the famous almond trees. She caught sight of the time and hurried to brush her teeth in the bathroom and pull on her clothes before Richard got back. She was just making the bed when his knock sounded on the door, and she sighed, considering it easier to leave her hair loose and her face as it was than risk his displeasure. She knotted the sleeves of her sweater round her shoulders, picked up her bag and opened the door to pass his waiting figure in silence. Richard took the bag from her and left it by the courtyard door, then led the way towards the stairs at the end of the hall. Harriet trailed unwillingly behind his tall figure down the stairs to the next floor where the scent of percolating coffee came from a big, modern kitchen. She took a hasty peep through the door of a dining-room with a table big enough for a banquet, and had time for only a glimpse of a large sitting-room before Richard hurried her towards wrought-iron gates which closed off the stairs to the floor below.

'To the dungeons, no doubt,' she said ruefully, but there was not the slightest flicker of response in his cold blue eyes as he closed the gates carefully and waved her on down the polished wood stairs.

'Incarceration is *not* something for you to worry about—at least, not here,' he added with a sinister smile.

The ground floor appeared to be solely a bedroom area, and led out to the patio with the pool Harriet had seen from the tower window. Richard knocked on one of the doors leading off the hall and a feminine voice called out permission to go in.

Harriet was stiff with sheer reluctance as Richard literally propelled her into the room ahead of him, and with a sinking feeling she looked from the young man propped up in the bed to the young woman, obviously related to him, sitting in a chair nearby. The two were very much alike, except for the sheen of health on the girl's dark hair, whereas the boy's fell dull and lank over a pale face with a newly-healed gash on the forehead. Two pairs of eyes of a softer, smokier blue than Richard's gazed at the newcomers with identical expressions of astonishment.

'Rico! When did *you* get here? We weren't expecting you for days yet!' exclaimed the boy, and Harriet glanced swiftly from his apprehensive face to the consternation in the eyes of the girl.

Richard pushed Harriet towards the foot of the bed. 'We arrived in the small hours, so I didn't come down here to disturb you. I left the surprise until this morning. As you can guess, *this* is Harriet Neil.' He turned to

Harriet in elaborate mock-courtesy. 'You've already met Penry Vaughan, of course, but this is his sister—and my sister-in-law—Katharine Livesey.'

'Oh, but Rico——' Kit started up from her chair in distress, but Richard held up a peremptory hand.

'I actually did manage to make off with Miss Neil—and gave her a taste of her own medicine, quite literally, by drugging her and then shutting her up in the Monteiro house before she came round. I won't say the trip was an unqualified success as a punishment, but I rather think the lady will hesitate before trying any of her little tricks again.'

Penry looked sick as he exchanged an anguished look with his white-faced sister.

'I—I don't know how to tell you this, Rico,' he said miserably, 'but in actual fact you've got the wrong girl!'

CHAPTER EIGHT

THE drive back to the Miramar shortly afterwards was accomplished in complete silence. Richard, looking like a man in shock, drove slowly and with great care, and Harriet sat motionless beside him, too drained of emotion to feel anything. According to Kit her husband, Reid, had rung only the night before to say that the police had the guilty girl in custody. She had been arrested during a drugs raid on a nightclub, and was found in possession of Penry's credit cards and his gold watch, and had eventually owned up to answering Penry's ill-fated advertisement, and to being with him in the car.

Richard's face had turned ashen as he listened to Kit, and the look in his eyes as he turned them on Harriet was one she would find hard to forget. The distress of the other two had been enough to arouse sympathy in her, but otherwise all she had felt was an overwhelming need to get away from all of them, to be on her own, and she had resisted urgent pleas to stay, merely asking Richard to take her back to the hotel as quickly as possible.

The atmosphere in the car was heavy with tension as Richard stopped the car in the Miramar's car-park. It was still very early, and no one was about as Harriet unclipped her seat-belt and waited apathetically for Richard to press the release-button on her door. Instead he turned in desperation and laid a hand on hers, and she flinched as though his touch revolted her.

'For God's sake don't jump away like that!' he said violently, and Harriet turned to stare at him in bleak surprise.

'What do you expect me to do—fall on your neck with gratitude now you consider me fit to bear you company?'

Richard closed his eyes momentarily, and swallowed. 'Just—just listen to me a moment. Please!' There was a rough note of despair in his voice that gave her fleeting satisfaction.

'Is there any reason why I should? You refused to listen to me when you carted me off to that haunted house of yours.' She kept her eyes fixed on the row of palms edging the car-park and missed the look of self-loathing on Richard's face.

'You have every right to be furious, Harriet—God knows you have. But I honestly believed you were the one——'

'Even though I told you over and over again that I wasn't?' she broke in cuttingly.

'You have to admit the evidence was against you,' he said heavily, and took out a cigar. 'May I?'

Harriet ignored him. 'How long do you intend keeping me here? I'm very tired.'

'Only a minute or two. I just want you to know why I felt so committed to a cause which I'm well aware you think was none of my concern anyway.'

'The reason seems fairly obvious to me now I've met her. You did it for your sister-in-law.'

'That's only a small part of it.' Richard rubbed his jaw wearily. 'When this all started my brother did the initial sleuthing, and traced you as far as your flat.'

Harriet turned startled eyes on him. 'You actually know where I live?'

He let out a cloud of smoke and nodded. 'At that point Reid had to fly to the States on business, so I volunteered to take over, to find out more about you.'

'You mean you had me *followed*?'

'No. I waited outside your flat in my car, for several evenings, in fact, until you came home. I'd watch you park that battered heap of yours and wait until you'd walked past me and gone into the building.'

'But why?' she asked, stunned.

'I wanted to see the original of that photograph—see you in the flesh, how you dressed, what sort of area you chose to live in.' Richard laughed shortly. 'It was difficult to see you properly because you were wearing one of those pull-on hats, then one night I struck lucky. The wind blew the hat off and your hair whipped out behind you like a flag, shining like a torch in the light from the street lamp, and you were laughing at the man with you as you ran into the house. I sat there smoking for some time, and was even luckier. You and your escort came out again and drove off and I followed you to the pub where both of you were obviously well known. I sat in a corner behind a rubber plant and watched you in the middle of a group of people, most of them men, and you were the centre of it. And after that I evolved my plan.'

Harriet watched him fixedly as he talked, the expression in her eyes changing from bewilderment to cold anger. 'You mean the sight of me was enough to make you kidnap me and drug me and frighten me to death in that mouldering old house? What kind of man *are* you, Richard Livesey? Is it only terrified women who turn you on? Were you the kind of child who pulled wings off flies?'

'For God's sake, Harriet, you've got it all wrong!' He

turned and seized her urgently by the shoulders. 'When I saw you clearly for the first time I was so bowled over by sheer anger and frustration I hardly knew how to stop myself from jumping out of the car to shake the truth out of you. What I'm trying to make you understand is that although I'm thirty-seven years old I had never in my whole life met a woman I wanted permanently—for the rest of my life. I envied Reid his happy marriage, but had resigned myself to permanent bachelorhood. Until I saw you. And you were everything I'd never even realised I was dreaming about. But you were also the one I believed had been involved with Penry and almost got him killed. Do you wonder I was angry?'

'With *me*?' Harriet tried to free herself, her unnatural composure cracking at last. 'But I'd never done anything to you!'

Richard held her fast and bent his face to hers. 'Don't you see, Harriet? I was angry with fate, for leading me to the one woman I wanted only to find she was apparently rotten at the core! So I arranged the holiday and met you by "accident", and did my utmost to attract you to me.'

'You succeeded only too easily,' she said bitterly, and turned her head away.

'It was mutual,' he retorted grimly. 'The plan went like clockwork, except that when I got you up to the Monteiro house you coped so well with everything I threw at you. My plan had been not only to drug you and frighten you with the strange bedroom, but leave you to your own devices for days on end without anything to read; no bath, no exercise, no entertainment, with the most ethnic meals Isabel could devise as a further trial. It was all so feasible in theory.' He slumped back into his seat. 'But I couldn't keep it up. I just couldn't leave you alone—in more ways than one.'

'Which brings us to the interesting part,' she said with venom. 'Why exactly *did* you make love to me?'

'Because I couldn't help myself!' he bit back savagely. 'It would never have happened if you hadn't screamed.

But once there in the room, with you in my arms, I hadn't a hope in hell. I lost my head.'

Harriet eyed him analytically. 'Tell me one more thing—then you can open this door and let me out of your life for good.'

'What do you want to know?'

'Before that last night you seemed to thaw considerably. Your manner could hardly be described as warm, but you were very definitely not hostile any more. But after—after you made love to me you treated me like dirt. Why?'

Richard winced and the lines round his mouth deepened. 'I had begun to believe in your innocence before I came to your room that night. I'd found nothing in your luggage that pointed towards the life the real girl must lead. No drugs—no pills or medication of any kind. You don't even smoke. So, almost against my will, I began to trust you. Then in the cold light of day afterwards—after that night with you—my mind pointed out something my brain had overlooked in the heat of the moment. It seemed fairly conclusive that only a woman with a wide and intensive experience of my sex could have responded with such a pagan absence of inhibition. And I'm damn fool enough to want someone less— less——'

'Secondhand?' supplied Harriet with sick distaste, and sat up very straight. 'I think that's enough for one day for anyone. Please open the door.'

Without another word Richard released the door catch and got out of the car to unlock the boot and take out her bag. The car-park was no longer deserted. Guests were beginning to emerge from the hotel, bent on the day's diversions, most of them laden with golf-clubs. Harriet took her bag from Richard and gave him a brief, social smile for the benefit of any curious eyes on them.

'I'll let you go now,' she said curtly.

'Harriet, please——' He half-moved towards her, then checked, deterred by the look on her face.

'No more, Richard,' she said flatly. 'Or do you prefer Rico?'

'It's a childhood name that stuck.'

Harriet put up a hand. 'Spare me the explanation. I'm not in the least interested in learning anything more about you than I already know.' A strand of bright hair flew across her face and she brushed it away impatiently. 'One more thing. If you could steer clear of this particular corner of the Algarve until I leave I'd be very grateful. Goodbye.'

She turned on her heel and left him without a backward glance, walking without haste to the hotel entrance to push her way through the revolving door in a haze of misery and fatigue. It took considerable effort to summon a smile for the friendly receptionist, who welcomed her back with a smile and expressed the hope that Harriet had enjoyed her trip. Harriet assured her it had been most interesting, and confirmed that she would be dining in the hotel that night.

Tonight and every night, thought Harriet as she went up in the lift, and shut herself in her room to give way at last to the tears she had been too proud to shed in front of Richard. She stayed in her room until dinner-time, sorely tempted to order dinner in her room, but resisted the temptation and got ready for dinner, putting on a plain black crêpe dress and the double strand of pearls her parents had given her for her twenty-first birthday. Mourning for a ruined holiday, she thought derisively as she looked at her reflection, and added extra make-up to disguise her heavy eyes and pallid face.

The Armstrongs were at their table when Harriet went in to dinner, and she smiled brightly in response to their animated welcome. Her dinner seemed more difficult to get through than usual, and she was only halfway through her main course when they passed her table on their way to the coffee lounge.

'Come and join us,' said Jane, and winked. 'Unless you've got a better offer!'

Harriet laughed and shook her head, wondering how she could explain Richard's absence for the remainder of the holiday since his attentions had been so marked for the first part of it. Perhaps she could say he'd gone back to Brazil—only they would be sure to run into him somewhere, which would be awkward. A pared-down version of the truth was the best thing—that there had been a quarrel, and that would be that.

Harriet was reluctant to leave the dining-room, not looking forward to her meeting with the Armstrongs, and loitered in the passageway leading from the dining-room to the foyer. She looked at the pieces of crystal displayed in the cases lining one wall, and one in particular caught her eye—a little crystal horse which had a look of Menina, and Harriet's throat thickened and she walked away quickly, so quickly she failed to see the man waiting for her in the foyer until she was almost in front of him. What little colour there had been in Harriet's face drained away as she came face to face with Richard. He looked elegant in a formal dark suit, but his eyes were bloodshot in his haggard face, and Harriet's instinct was to turn tail and run, but there were people moving round them in all directions, and she shrank from making herself conspicuous.

'Good evening, Harriet.' He gestured towards the bar. 'May I buy you a drink?'

Harriet looked at him in disbelief. 'No, you may not. I thought I'd made my feelings quite clear this morning.' Her mouth tightened as she clamped down on the black anger that rose inside her like boiling pitch at the mere sight of him.

A pulse throbbed at the corner of Richard's mouth as he held out a large envelope. 'I omitted to give you these this morning, or I wouldn't have troubled you. Your passport and papers,' he added.

'Oh.' She stared blindly at the envelope as she took it from him. 'I forgot about them too. Thank you, though you needn't have troubled to deliver them in person. You could have left them for me at the desk.'

'I know. But I wanted to see you.'

'Why?'

'To apologise, to grovel,' he said without emphasis. 'In short, do anything that might change your feelings towards me.'

'Nothing will change those, I'm afraid.' Which, thought Harriet bleakly, was the honest truth.

Richard's face grew strained. 'I'd give anything to alter what's happened, Harriet——'

'Since that's impossible let's forget it. All of it,' she said deliberately. 'Thank you so much for bringing my things. I'll say goodbye, since I don't suppose we shall run into each other again. I'm leaving at the weekend.'

'I leave for the north again tomorrow, unfortunately. Isabel has been taken ill, according to Helio when I rang, and I feel I should go up to see her.'

'I'm sorry,' said Harriet stiffly. 'Please give her my best wishes for her recovery.'

'Please, Harriet!' He glanced around and took her by the elbow. 'I must talk to you alone for a moment. Walk with me to the car—it's too public here.'

Short of making a scene there seemed nothing Harriet could do in view of the grip he had on her arm, and with her face burning with resentment she let herself be ushered through the revolving door to walk with Richard in silence to the deserted car-park. She stopped as they reached the car and demanded, 'Well?'

'I wouldn't leave tomorrow if Isabel weren't ill——'

'Just a minute—does Isabel have a telephone, then?' interrupted Harriet.

'Yes. She lives in the village near the Vinha Monteiro, in a nice little house with modern plumbing, electric light and a gas cooker—*and* a telephone.' Richard's voice was warily apologetic. 'Which is why she so strongly disaproved of the way you were shut up at the old house.'

'I see. Does she know why?'

'She thinks I was keeping you there to persuade you to marry me.'

'How ludicrous!'

'Not to Isabel—nor to me,' he added so quietly Harriet wondered if she'd heard him correctly.

'Do I take it that you find the thought of me as a wife remotely acceptable?' she asked with scorn. 'I thought your requirements specified a brand-new model with no previous mileage, not someone like me!'

Without warning he caught her by the arms and drew her rigid body towards him. 'I'm past caring about that any more,' he said hoarsely. 'All I know, or care about, is that you're the one woman in the world I want, and as long as I'm the only man in your life as of now I don't care a damn how many men there were before me——'

'How frightfully magnanimous of you!' she spat, and tore herself from his grasp.

'Don't, Harriet—please——' and Richard jerked her into his arms and kissed her hungrily. At the touch of his lips Harriet's knees gave involuntarily, and his arms tightened in triumph as he held her closer. 'I'll be back well before you leave—God, I wish I didn't have to go,' he muttered against her mouth. 'Wait for me, darling——'

'I'll do nothing of the kind—what do you take me for!' Harriet was beside herself with rage as she jumped back, still clutching her envelope. 'As far as I'm concerned you can go back to Minho, or to hell, and stay there. You've done such irreparable damage to me and my life, and you have the colossal nerve to imagine all you have to do is kiss it better? Not on your life, Mr Livesey! I never want to set eyes on you again. Ever!'

Blind to the desperation on Richard's face, she spun on her heel and made rapidly for the hotel and the sanctuary of her room, staying there until she was calm enough to join the Armstrongs.

Harriet's parting shot at Richard was sheer angry

bravado. For every minute of the rest of her stay in Praia
do Ceu she wanted to see him so badly it was like a
physical pain nothing could relieve. It was a nightmare to
see everyone else in the hotel so tanned and full of
bonhomie while she lay by the pool trying to pick up the
pieces of her shattered private world. Only her raw anger
helped her in the resolve to put Richard out of her life,
forget him completely, and endlessly she tried to think of
some retaliation she could make, however childish and
petty. There seemed only one thing possible; to pay him
back the money he'd laid out on her holiday—throw it in
his face as a gesture that would satisfy just a little her
crying need for revenge, and hopefully get him on the
raw. So Richard Livesey was willing to take her with all
faults, was he! Harriet's eyes flashed at the thought. How
exceedingly generous! Marriage had never been mentioned, of course—the abject apologies had been one
great big con to wheedle himself back into her bed,
regardless of the estimated number of previous occu-
pants. Hot, salt tears slid down behind Harriet's sunglasses as she remembered, for the hundredth time, the
night in the Monteiro bed. For Richard it had probably
just been one of any number of similar experiences, while
for Harriet Neil, prize fool, it had been the supreme
moment of her life.

Harriet's tears dried on her hot cheeks as she thought
of the culprit responsible for the whole stupid mix-up
right at the start. She would discover the identity of the
practical joker who had sent her photograph to Penry if it
took forever, though somehow she had a fair idea it
would be a lot sooner than that once she got back to the
Acme Mail Order Company. And when she did Harvey
Jackson would get an earful too—*and* her notice thrown
in his face! From now on Harriet Neil would be pushed
around no more; by Richard, Harvey or anyone else in
the world. It was *her* turn to do the pushing. And while
she was about it, she would find out who had taken *her*
identity and *her* good name and used them without

thought for anything except 'having a good time'.

Harriet's first course of action on her return to work was
to act on her hunch and march into the typing pool to
demand in no uncertain terms the identity of the charmer
who had sent her photograph in answer to the
advertisement. It was laughably easy to identify the
culprit. Every pair of eyes in the room swivelled
automatically to Hazel Bishop, who flushed a bright
crimson that clashed horribly with her hair and admitted
her guilt immediately. In response to Harriet's third
degree she told her little tale miserably. Harriet had
dropped her handbag in the cloakroom one day and
Hazel had helped her pick up the contents, finding the
snapshot on the floor afterwards, and on impulse she had
pocketed it. Her elder sister Tracey, the one who was
going to be the next Joan Collins and was meanwhile
filling in as a model for the Acme Mail Order Catalogue,
had dropped in the same afternoon to show Hazel
Penry's advertisement and to ask her to type Tracey's
answer. There had been only one drawback—Tracey had
just dyed her hair from pink and green streaks to a less
alarming blonde, and had no photograph to send with the
letter.

It had just been a joke to send Harriet's photograph
with the letter, she insisted frantically. Tracey and she
were about the same height, Tracey's new hair was very
similar to Harriet's. And because of the name 'Harry' on
the back of the photograph, they'd had to use Harriet's
name to sign the letter . . . Tracey, they'd reasoned, was
quite capable of dealing with any objections from Box
1348—always assuming he cared that his companion
wasn't actually called Harriet Neil.

She asked what Harriet meant to do, her eyes like
saucers with apprehension. Tracey was already in
trouble with the police 'over there', and their dad was
furious . . . Harriet had the impression that the latter was
the worst part of it all in Hazel's eyes. To her own

considerable surprise Harriet suddenly found she had no urge to do anything very much, and merely gave Hazel a short, sharp lecture on the criminal irresponsibility of her and her sister's behaviour. She harrowed Hazel's feelings with hints of prosecution, then relieved them by agreeing to let the matter drop.

Flushed with success, Harriet then went straight in to beard Harvey Jackson in his den and handed him her notice, informing him in no uncertain terms of her opinion of men who accepted large bribes from strange men to lure innocent girls, and what his fellow Rotarians might think if she published his involvement. She watched with deep satisfaction as he turned a sickly shade of grey and insisted that he had genuinely thought he was doing her a favour. Harriet told him politely what he could do with his favours, and let him know she would require four weeks' wages despite the fact that she was leaving his employ as of that moment, which hurt Harvey where he felt it most—in his wallet.

Half an hour later she had shaken the dust of the Acme Mail Order Company from her feet for ever, the richer by four weeks' wages which she would have loved to throw in Harvey Jackson's face if she hadn't had a specific purpose for the money. It was going towards what she thought of as her revenge fund. When she got back into town she put an advertisement in the local paper regarding the sale of her car, then began the search for another job. To her great surprise one was available immediately, and she was sent along to the local department store for an interview for the privilege of selling weird clothes to teenagers in Poppy's, the new boutique that had been opened on the second floor. Despite the large number of other applicants Harriet was given the job, more due to her experience in previous work than her suitability as a sales person, and because the store manager seemed to think her hair was eye-catching and would attract the type of customer he wanted. Harriet took the job thankfully, afraid to let it slip in the hope of finding something more suited to her training, and comforted herself with the thought that she could keep on looking for another job while she was working—and earning money, which was her main objective.

Harriet spent a weekend with her parents to deliver the presents brought back for them, and endured a catechism on her change of job, giving the flippant, though perfectly truthful, reason of being unable to stand working for Harvey Jackson another minute. A few days later an evening was spent with Guy and Delia telling the same tale, though all the members of her family were plainly disturbed by a certain feverish gaiety Harriet assumed to hide the unhappiness beneath it.

'Tell me what's wrong, darling,' said Mrs Neil, and Harriet gave way to tears in her mother's arms, but quickly pulled herself together and laughed and assured her parents it was nothing to worry about, just a holiday romance, refusing to talk further on the subject.

Delia was less tactful than her parents-in-law.

'Some man on holiday, was it?' she demanded, and her husband groaned and told her to mind her own business.

'I feel it *is* my business—and yours—when Harriet looks so tired and scrawny, apart from the odd goings on like chucking in her job and selling her car,' retorted Delia. 'Something's obviously wrong. Not pregnant, are you, Harriet?'

Guy groaned even louder and his sister went bright red.

'No, I'm not,' she said emphatically. 'I needed some money in a hurry, which is why I sold the car, and I left my job because I couldn't stick another day with Harvey.'

Guy looked perturbed. 'So why do you need money? Can we help?'

Harriet smiled at him gratefully. 'That's very sweet of you, but no thanks. I'm saving up for a holiday in Portugal.'

The other two stared at her open-mouthed.

'But you've just had one,' pointed out Delia.

'I know. That's the one I'm saving up for.'

A few days later the first letter arrived from Richard. Harriet eyed it coldly and almost sent it back unopened, but curiosity won the day. She kicked off her shoes from feet that ached badly from long hours spent supporting her in her new job, and sat down to read what he said.

He had tried to get back to Praia do Ceu before she left, he wrote, but poor old Isabel had needed hospitalisation, and by the time he had assured himself that all was well with her it was too late to try to see Harriet again.

'She kept saying something about your sheets over and over again,' he wrote, 'until I finally realised the significance of what she was telling me.' Harriet stiffened and went hot all over as she read on. 'I have no words to express my feelings. I can only plead your forgiveness for my ignorance of the miraculous gift I received without even realising the full extent of its worth.'

With unsteady hands Harriet made a note of the address in her book, put the letter in another envelope and addressed it to Richard without an accompanying word. In the weeks that followed two more letters came, but Harriet returned these without reading them, and meanwhile practised stringent economies in her life-style to save money as fast as she possibly could. She found out the cost of her holiday at the Miramar from a travel agency, and with the money from Harvey Jackson, plus the sum from the sale of her car, Harriet had the necessary amount five weeks from the time of her return from Portugal. She made out a cheque to Richard and sent it to him with a terse note: 'Reimbursement for air flight and two weeks' vacation at Hotel Miramar. H. Neil.'

She posted the letter in her lunch-hour and worked for the rest of the day buoyed up by a deep sense of malicious satisfaction not even the end-of-season sale in the boutique could mar. But as she walked home that evening reaction set in. The glow had faded, leaving her vaguely depressed and out of sorts, and though she went out later with a group of friends to the local for an hour, the flat, listless feeling persisted. It kept on persisting for several days. Harriet thought about ringing Guy and Delia to invite herself to lunch the following Sunday, but decided against it as unfair to saddle them with her company until she had bucked herself up a bit. Then one day she was intercepted by the elderly lady who lived in the flat next to hers. A large box had come by carrier for Harriet and Miss Jarman had taken it in, knowing her young neighbour was out all day. The box was large, and after thanking Miss Jarman Harriet had quite a struggle to heave it into her living-room to open it. Once she had prized open the box and pulled out all the packing and polystyrene chips inside she lifted out a foam-wrapped object and unwrapped it with care. It was the exquisite ceramic of fruits and vegetables she had yearned over in the little shop in Praia do Ceu. She gazed at it in silence, its vibrant colours shimmering through a haze of tears, then she laid it down with care before searching for the card she felt certain must be with it. She found it at last and tore open the envelope with shaking fingers, swallowing hard as she read the familiar script. It said quite simply, 'With my love, always, Richard.'

Harriet crumpled in a heap on the floor, clutching the card to her chest as she cried her eyes out. It was some time before she recovered sufficiently to clear away the box and wrappings and take down her Hockney print to hang up the ceramic on the only strong picture-hook in the flat in its place. After a snack she sat down to compose a thank-you letter, but for some reason it was impossible to find words to put down on the blank sheet. She left it until the following day, but the same mental block resulted in sheet after sheet of paper being screwed into balls and thrown away in disgust after reading the stilted words she had managed to get down. She still hadn't achieved success when she received her bank statement a few days later and saw the two eye-catching items on it. One was the cheque paid out to Richard, and a few items later exactly the same amount had been paid back into her account. Harriet blinked, and looked again, but there was no mistake. Richard had promptly paid the money back into her bank instead of returning her cheque.

Whoever said revenge was sweet was a fool, she thought drearily that night, as she lay tossing and turning in her bed. All it had done for her was make her unhappy, and very sorry she had ever tried to take revenge on Richard. A pretty abortive revenge it had turned out to be, too, she reflected sadly, except that in some strange way it had purged her of all the anger and resentment she had felt towards Richard and left her with only the love she had felt for him almost from the beginning. The only shred of comfort she had was anticipation of his next letter, which she would read with eagerness when it came.

No other letter ever arrived, however. The present of the ceramic bore all the hallmarks of a parting gift, and Harriet finally became convinced Richard had given up on her. The prospect brought a steely look to her eye. If Richard imagined everything was all over he was sadly mistaken. *She* wasn't going to give up so easily—in fact, she decided, she would go back to Praia do Céu post-haste and tell him—tell him . . . Harriet frowned and bit her lip. She was a bit uncertain as to her exact words to him yet, unless he was interested in hearing that her life was a wasteland without him. Now that Harriet's hurt and outrage had subsided she could see the truth with simple clarity. She loved and wanted Richard so much that if it just meant sharing his life—and his bed—for only a while, so be it, that was exactly what she'd do. She had never wanted to share anyone else's up to now, and after meeting Richard it seemed more than likely she never would again, either, which made wasting her life in pointless regrets seem a fairly pointless exercise.

Ah, but what if he doesn't want *you*? asked her nagging brain. She shrugged. In that case she would come back to Leamington—or even go to Norwich—and get on with the rest of her life the best way she could. But to leave things the way they were was insupportable. What an idiot she'd been to send his other letters back unopened—she should have given him a hearing at least—but it was too late to think about that now. Her only course of action was to make for the Algarve as soon as she could and put an end to this soul-destroying uncertainty. Harriet sighed. It would have been easier on her ego if Richard had come to *her*, but after getting his money thrown back in his face and his letters returned unopened it was small wonder he thought she wanted nothing more to do with him, whereas in actual fact she wanted him so much it was worth pocketing her pride to board the first available plane just to see his face again.

Before she could change her mind Harriet went to the travel agency next day and asked for the first possible reservation at the Hotel Miramar. There was nothing until December, she was told—in fact the only thing available was a small studio apartment, due to a cancellation. It was behind the church, had no sea view, but the booking was for the following two weeks and she jumped at it joyfully, then hurried back to the store in a state of euphoria to charm the manager into giving her the necessary time off for the trip.

CHAPTER NINE

THE small one-room apartment with bath in the Edificio Beira Mar was a far cry from the Hotel Miramar, but Harriet was so glad to be actually in Praia do Ceu, and within reach of Richard at last, she thanked the janitor gratefully as he let her in, and unpacked swiftly, then took a shower before hurrying out again to the taxi-rank in the *praça*. She persuaded the taxi-driver to take her to Vale do Centianes and sat in the back of the car in a fever of anticipation as she came nearer to meeting Richard again, praying he would be glad to see her, not even letting herself contemplate the possibility that he might not. In any case, however he felt about her now she just had to see him and talk to him, if only for a little while, to tell him that all thoughts of revenge and anger had long since left her to leave the field clear for the love that had been stronger than either of them all along if only she had been able to see it. Harriet bit her lip at the thought of the unopened letters, and the sight of Torre Branca as the car jolted up the drive towards it threw her into an advanced state of nerves by the time she got out of the car to knock on the door after asking the driver to wait for her.

It seemed a very long time before the door finally opened, and a young girl stood looking at Harriet in enquiry.

'*Boa tarde, senhora,*' she said politely.

Harriet smiled nervously. 'Good afternoon. Is Mr Livesey in?'

The girl spread her hands in regret. '*Nao, senhora. Senhor Ricardo foi embora ontem.*'

Harriet's heart sank, and she stared at the girl in frustration, then turned and beckoned the taxi-driver, asking him if he could act as interpreter. With the aid of

168

his sketchy English he was able to translate the quick-fire conversation he had with the girl, who told him the house was empty and that Senhor Ricardo had left the day before. Harriet thanked the girl and the driver automatically and got back in the car, feeling numb. She stared through the window on the journey back, blind to the charm of Vale do Centianes, or of Carvoeiro as they passed through it, not even nervous of the speed at which the driver tore back along the main highway to Praia do Ceu. How stupid she had been, thought Harriet in misery. It had just never occurred to her that Richard would have gone back to Brazil, though to miss him by a mere day seemed cruel in the extreme. No doubt he had told her in his letters if she could have come down from her high horse sufficiently to read them. But she had *not* read them, and now she had only herself to blame for being obliged to spend two weeks alone in that tiny room in the Beira Mar. In the Miramar, at least, there had been other people around, and somewhere to dine each evening. This time things would be vastly different. In all ways.

The days dragged by at a snail's pace. Harriet felt unequal to the prospect of dining in a restaurant at night alone, so she shopped in the supermarket for food each day and ate a solitary salad in the evening, then read until it was late enough to go to bed. The days she spent on the beach, venturing off it to the café nearby to eat an omelette or freshly caught fish, and wandered round the shops, though the only money she felt justified in spending was on more paperback novels to read in the evenings. She went early to bed, which also, unfortunately, meant early to rise, and Harriet found it difficult to stay in bed very late. She went early to the shops each day and bought fresh rolls and a day-old English newspaper, taking them back to her room to while away an hour over coffee before she tidied up and went down to the beach again. The weather was perfect, yet in some odd way the bright sunlight and cerulean blue sea only seemed to

intensify the heaviness of her heart. She laughed
inwardly at her own naïveté in expecting Richard to
be waiting for her with open arms, and almost looked
forward to being home again and back in the routine of
her humdrum existence once more.

She spent the third morning on the beach with a book
as usual, but after grilled sardines in her usual café spent
only a short time looking round the shops, most of which
were closed at that time, which was easier on her purse.
Afterwards for the first time she allowed herself to
wander farther afield, and went on towards the quay
with the tiny chapel that overlooked the harbour. She
leaned against the wall and gazed at the boats drawn up
on the sand, wondering if the one Richard had been
mending was among them. Restlessly she began to walk
along the road past the harbour, hardly realising how far
she'd gone until she saw the restaurant where Richard
had taken her for their first meal together. Her teeth
caught in her lower lip and she sighed. What an idiot she
had been to come back here! Everything reminded her of
Richard. It would be a relief to get back home to drizzle
and fog and the slight comfort of things familiar.

Suddenly her stomach lurched and she stopped dead
for a moment before dodging behind a carousel of
postcards outside a souvenir shop. She blinked rapidly,
hardly able to believe her eyes, but the car coming to a
halt outside the Restaurant Alba Mar a short distance
away was a white Mercedes which looked remarkably
like Richard's. A second later she was quite sure, as
Richard jumped from the car to help out a dark young
woman in a honey-coloured silk dress which did full
justice to her generously curved figure. Harriet watched,
stricken, as Richard took the lady by the arm, smiling
down at her as he went with her into the restaurant.

Harriet walked back to her apartment in a daze, trying
to take in the fact that not only had Richard stayed here
instead of going back to Brazil, but he was very happily
occupied, judging by his beautiful companion. It had

been one thing to think he was in Brazil and she would never see him again, but to see him in the flesh, actually here in Praia do Ceu outside the restaurant he'd taken her for their first meal, and with another woman—a very attractive woman at that—was totally unbearable. Harriet raced up the two flights of stairs to her room as though demons were at her heels, and once inside threw herself on the narrow bed face down and let black misery close over her head and leave her to drown in its depths. Time passed unheeded as she lay there motionless, suspended in her misery like a fly in amber, until finally the tears began to flow, soaking the roots of her hair and making her T-shirt damp. Then even the tears dried, and she was left with a burning face and swollen eyes, too apathetic to get up to splash herself with cold water. All she could think about was that she had eleven days before she could get on a plane and escape. What could she *do* with herself? she thought in a frenzy, and plucked wildly at her hair, which spread in an untidy mess over the bed. If Richard were here she might meet him any time she went outside her room. And the prospect of that under the present circumstances was so mortifying she curled up in an anguished ball at the mere thought. Suddenly she jumped out of her skin as someone began to hammer on the door. She stayed where she was, not making a sound, hoping that whoever it was would go away again. Then her heart thumped madly as Richard's voice shouted,

'Harriet! Let me in. I know you're in there—the janitor says you haven't left since you came back after lunch.' There was a pause, then 'Harriet! I'll break the door down,' he threatened.

Harriet rubbed futilely at her eyes and opened the door unwillingly, glaring at Richard as he brushed past her and slammed the door shut behind him.

'What the hell are you doing *here*?' he demanded angrily.

'*I* should be the one asking that,' she snapped. 'This is

my room—why shouldn't I be here?' She peered past him pointedly. 'Are you alone?'

'What are you talking about? Of course I'm alone!' Richard stared down at her, angry colour flaring in his face as he raked a hand through his hair. 'What I meant was what are you doing here in Praia do Ceu?'

'Trying to enjoy the holiday that was wrecked for me last time—not that it's any of your concern!'

'Everything you do is my concern. Do you realise I've been off my head with worry trying to find out where you were? I've been racing all over Leamington like a lunatic searching for someone who knew where you were.'

'*Leamington!*' Harriet's mouth dropped open inelegantly as she stared at him in astonishment. 'You've been to *Leamington*?'

'That's where you live, isn't it?' he asked irritably. 'I spoke to the woman who lives in the flat next door to yours and she said you'd gone away but she had no idea where. Then Harvey Jackson told me you resigned from your job the first day you went back, and I was stumped. I had no idea where your brother or your parents lived, and I had to give up after a while as I had to be back here by today anyway——'

'For something important?' asked Harriet sweetly.

Richard frowned. 'Yes. Quite important, anyway. What made you say that?'

'Oh, nothing,' she said airily, and leaned casually against the wash-basin.

'Harriet——' he began, and caught her roughly by the elbows, hesitating as he looked down at her flushed face and swollen eyes. 'You've been crying,' he said accusingly.

'No, I haven't.' She struggled to get free, but his grip tightened. 'A touch of the sun, that's all.'

'You're lying!'

'And you would know, of course—you're so good at lying yourself!' This time she succeeded in pulling free and stood glaring at him in resentment, not a little of which was due to his appearance. He looked so overpoweringly attractive and elegant in biscuit linen trousers and cream lawn shirt, while she—Harriet shuddered at the thought of her appearance.

'What is it?' he asked sharply.

'I look a mess,' she blurted, and her pink cheeks coloured even more as he inspected her from head to foot. He took his time, his eyes travelling slowly from the tangled mane of hair to her swollen face, then lingering on the damp, clinging T-shirt before moving down over the length of her legs from her brief shorts to her bare feet. Her toes curled involuntarily, and he looked up again.

'Harriet,' he said gently, 'you've been crying your eyes out—it's quite useless to deny it. Why?'

'I have not,' she insisted, then something occurred to her. 'Just exactly how did you find out I was here?'

'I've just been to the Miramar and one of the receptionists told me she'd seen you coming into this building when she was on her way to work after lunch.' Richard stood with arms folded, and smiled wryly. 'I told her she was seeing things, but she was quite definite. You took your sunhat off as you ran past her into the building and she saw your hair.'

'My hair,' repeated Harriet bitterly, and clutched at it. 'Sometimes I think I'll cut it off and dye it another colour.'

'No!' He moved towards her involuntarily, then checked himself. 'That would be a tragedy.'

'There's a lot more to me than just hair,' she said angrily, and backed away as he moved towards her again.

'As I'm in a better position to know than most people,' he said deliberately.

Harriet's eyes flashed under their swollen lids. 'That's just the sort of remark I could have expected, I suppose—from a man like you.'

'And what kind of man am I?' he asked, his eyes glittering.

'One who believed I was a tramp—amongst other things.' Her mouth trembled and she bit her lip hard.

'If you had read my letters perhaps you might understand how much I regret what I thought, what I did—how much I'd give to be able to undo almost everything that happened between us and start again.' Richard moved nearer still, his eyes holding hers. 'I use the word "almost" intentionally, Harriet, because if I never see you again for the rest of my life I shall have had that one night with you.'

Her chin lifted. 'Such a pity your enthusiasm evaporated so completely by the following morning, though, isn't it?'

Richard gritted his teeth, letting out a deep breath. 'Why *are* you here, Harriet?' he asked. 'Tell me the truth.'

'I've already told you.'

'It seems strange to me that you chose to come back here, when you could have gone practically anywhere else. Yet you came to the place where it was almost certain you'd meet me again.'

'But Richard,' she said gently, 'I naturally assumed you would have gone back to Brazil by now. After all, you told me you were staying in Torre Branca with friends— or was that a lie, too?'

'Only partly,' he answered gravely. 'Torre Branca belongs to me, and I live here in the Algarve now. But I wasn't lying when I said I lived in Brazil. I did; all my life until recently.' Richard looked about him with distaste. 'Harriet, there's so much I want to say—to explain, but we can't talk here. Have dinner with me—please. I refuse to believe that you've come here without the intention of at least giving me a hearing.'

'Won't the lady you took to lunch object?' retorted Harriet rashly, and could have bitten her tongue out as she watched the blank look on Richard's face change swiftly to comprehension, and something more than that; something she disliked the look of very much.

'You saw me with Adalgisa?' he said blandly, and sat down on the room's solitary chair. He leaned back, relaxed, and smiled at her. 'She's a lovely creature, isn't she?'

'I didn't notice,' lied Harriet. 'I was on my way back here—I barely had time to realise it was you.'

'A pity you were in such a hurry,' he commented, 'or you'd have seen another car draw up behind mine, with José Oliveira and his wife and daughter, whom you might have recognised, also a man by the name of João Monteiro, a relative of mine. The lady with me was his wife, and the mother of his three sons.'

'Oh.' Harriet was besieged by several emotions all at once, notably embarrassment and sheer relief. 'It's nothing to do with me,' she said loftily.

Richard's eyes were very bright. 'Yet I'd lay odds that Adalgisa was the reason for your tears.'

She managed a little laugh. 'What nonsense! I don't know the lady—besides, I haven't *been* crying. It was too much sun, as I told you.'

'And I still say you're lying,' he said pleasantly, and stood up. 'No matter—now, are you dining with me, or are you about to indulge in your favourite pastime of saying no?'

Harriet was torn between pride, which prompted her to refuse, and instinct, which longed to accept. Richard was hatefully aware of her inner struggle by the amused look on his face.

'Well?' he prompted. '*Are* you going to say no?'

'No,' she answered, and for the first time gave him a faint smile. It prompted such a brilliant smile from him in return she backed away again involuntarily.

Richard chose to ignore her retreat and gave a disparaging glance at the room. 'I suppose there's no chance of waiting here while you get ready——'

'You want me to come *now*?'

'You bet your sweet life I do.' Richard opened the door and gave her a quizzical smile. 'Until we've cleared up a few little points between us, at least, I don't intend to let you out of my sight, Miss Neil. I'll be in the bar opposite—don't keep me waiting long. Twenty minutes should be enough, so get a move on.'

Harriet did as she was told, spending a precious five minutes under the shower with her hair bundled up into a plastic cap, letting the cool spray soothe her face. When she was dry she performed a small miracle of camouflage on her eyes with make-up, then brushed her hair until it crackled and hung down her back in a shining mass. Finally she dived into the sundress she had made for herself only the week before in navy cotton jersey striped boldly in pale yellow, quite pleased with herself at the skilful cut of the halter neck and the full skirt. A final spray of perfume and she was ready at the precise moment Richard knocked on the door again.

'Time's up, Harriet!' he yelled, and she threw open the door, scowling.

'There *are* other people in the building!' she snapped, but he shrugged carelessly, grinning as she locked the door.

'I'm sure they'll have every sympathy with my impatience—one look at you is enough.' His eyes were alight with approval, and something else. Something that made her heart skip a beat. 'Are you the same girl I left a few minutes ago? You look delectable.'

Harriet gave him a wry look as she preceded him down the stairs. 'Slightly back-handed, as compliments go, but thank you just the same.'

They were in the car and on their way out of Praia do Ceu when she thought to ask him where he was taking her.

'Home,' he informed her.

'To Torre Branca? Or do you have some other place several hundreds of miles away? I mean, should I have brought a toothbrush?' she asked, tartly.

'Unnecessary—I always keep a spare,' he assured her blandly. 'But you were right about Torre Branca.'

Harriet frowned, in something of a quandary as she wondered whether she should tell him about her recent abortive visit there, then remembered the maid, who had probably told him already, anyway.

'Did you know that I went to Torre Branca on Sunday?' she asked reluctantly.

'No.' Richard shot her a surprised look. 'How did you get there?'

'By taxi. Your maid said you'd gone away, and I concluded you'd gone back to Brazil.'

'So you thought I'd given up, folded my tent, and stolen away for good.'

'Something like that.'

'And how did you feel about it?'

'Taken aback—and hideously embarrassed.'

'Which is all very lukewarm and unflattering. But then I thought you came back here for a holiday only because you thought I *had* gone back to Brazil.'

'No.' Harriet decided to come clean. 'It was a surprise when you paid the money back into my account. I haven't thanked you for it, I'm sorry.'

'It worried me like hell to think how you'd managed to get the money together,' he said heavily. 'Even more when I found you'd thrown in your job.'

'Yes, well—when I saw the entry on my bank statement I decided to use it for another holiday and come to see you to thank you for the beautiful present you sent me, and generally bury the hatchet.'

'Where—in my skull?'

She gave him a hostile glance. 'I'm trying to be nice, in case you hadn't noticed. Anyway, to continue; after sending you the cheque, petty little gesture though it was, I didn't feel bitter towards you any more, to my surprise.'

'How *did* you feel?' he asked instantly.

Harriet had no intention of letting him know that at this stage. 'I don't know. Perhaps that's why I came back here; to find out.'

Richard shook his head. 'Amazing, isn't it? For week
I'd stuck it out, hoping you'd thaw, particularly after Ki
and Reid took the ceramic back to England and sent it t
you for me. But still nothing, so I decided to take off t
the U.K. to see you, and of course it was at that exac
point that you flew in the opposite direction.'

At that moment he turned the car off the road to clim
up the steep drive, and Harriet was saved from a direc
answer by commenting on the long, paved stretc
leading to the house. 'This must have cost you quite
bit—I can see it's been recently done,' she said. 'Why i
there a narrow grass track right up the middle of it?'

'You may well ask!' he laughed, and brought the car t
a halt in the courtyard. 'The damn *calcada*—the pave
bit—cost an arm and a leg, partly because by law I wa
obliged to leave a muletrack running down it.'

'How lovely!' Harriet smiled at him as they went to th
door together, her face sobering as she thought of the sic
disappointment of her previous arrival.

'What is it?' he asked, quick to sense her change c
mood.

'I was thinking of the last time I came—and found yo
gone.'

'You said you just felt embarrassed.'

'I felt a lot more than that—disappointed, deflated—
lots of things really.'

'Were you sorry?' His blue eyes held hers steadily.

'Yes,' said Harriet simply, and followed him as he le
the way into the house, past the bedroom she had slept i
and on down the stairs to the big room she had onl
glimpsed briefly before.

'This is my only real sitting-room,' he said. 'I enlarge
an existing room, extending it outwards to make the mos
of the view, and decided to use toughened glass for th
entire wall. Not to everyone's taste, actually—Reid say
it's like sitting in a goldfish bowl.'

'I like it,' said Harriet, and looked with warm approva

t the panoramic view, then at the furnishings, which
vere in no particular style, with dark, carved cabinets
nd tables alongside velvet-covered chairs and a leather
hesterfield sofa, but the general effect was of great
omfort, and appealed to her very much.

'Some of the things came from my parents' home,
thers I've bought for myself—what do you think?' asked
Richard.

'I think it's a welcoming, warm room,' she said
incerely, and he smiled brilliantly and turned to one of
he cabinets.

'Let's have a drink.' He opened a bottle with a loud
op and poured the foaming contents into two glasses,
anding one to Harriet. 'What shall we drink to—better
nderstanding?'

'Amen to that,' she said solemnly, and sipped the wine,
er eyebrows lifting. 'Now this tastes rather more French
han Portuguese, even to my inexperienced palate. Surely
t's vintage champagne. Are we celebrating?'

'I am certainly!' Richard led her to the sofa. 'Let's sit
ere and watch the sun go down, and afterwards I'll see
vhat Rosa has left in the fridge for dinner.'

'Is Rosa the young girl I saw on Sunday?' asked
Harriet, and relaxed against the squabbed leather.

He frowned. 'Rosa's getting on a bit, actually.
'robably that was Maria, her daughter, who has her
ead so full of her forthcoming wedding I suppose she
orgot to tell Rosa you were here.'

'It doesn't matter.'

'It does to me, Harriet,' he said emphatically, and
opped up her glass.

Harriet had nothing to say in answer to that. 'Tell me
vhy you don't live in Brazil any more,' she said, without
ooking at him, and Richard smiled a little, and leaned
ack on the other corner of the sofa.

'Two years ago, not long after Reid and Kit got
narried, my parents died within a couple of months of
ach other. After that I grew lonely and restless, and to

cut a long story short I called Reid over and we decided
put the *fazenda* up for sale. I had a neighbour who'd bee
after the property for years and it all went through fair
quickly. I put most of my share of the money in th
marina you've seen already in Praia do Ceu. Reid's
merchant banking, and has been tremendously helpful
me in getting things started, and he's put some of his ow
capital into it as well as persuading José Oliveira fro
the Miramar to do the same, while I worked on o
Monteiro relatives from Viana do Castelo. I own th
major share and will be concerned with the running
the marina once it's finished, and today was the day v
all finally cemented the venture with a celebratory lunc
The Monteiros were represented by João, who's the mo
interested, being a marine engineer, and of course l
brought his very charming wife Adalgisa down last nig'
with him. They had to return to day because of th
children, hence a lunch instead of dinner. Reid is tied u
in Brussels unexpectedly on business, so he couldn
make it.'

Harriet took some time to digest this. 'So you're not
farmer any more,' she said after a time.

'It was a loose description at best.'

'Won't you miss the life?'

Richard looked away through the great window. '1
some ways, I suppose, but latterly things had grow
difficult anyway, and in the end I was very glad to leave

'Difficult economically, you mean?' asked Harrie
curiously.

'Socially rather.' He looked a little uncomfortabl
'Enrique Perreira, our nearest neighbour, died not lon
before my parents. He was only forty and his death cam
as a shock to his wife Ana, who was ten years younge
and very ambitious. She was the one who wanted ou
land. Unfortunately she was also on the lookout for
second husband——'

'Which is where you came in,' said Harriet, with
gleam in her eye.

'Precisely. It all seemed very logical to her, but not, I'm afraid to me, so as I couldn't stand the heat I got out of the kitchen, so to speak.'

'Is she beautiful?'

Richard turned thoughtful eyes on her. 'Yes, I suppose she is. Lots of black hair, huge eyes, very imperious; rules her children and her household with a rod of iron—a real *dona da casa*. But my taste runs to yellow hair and—well——'

'You'd much prefer your bride to be brand-new at the job,' Harriet finished for him. 'Especially in bed.'

The ensuing silence was not as hostile as it would have been the previous time they met, but there was a very definite challenge in the dark eyes as they looked steadily into Richard's.

'Every man has his dream, however laughable it may seem to others,' he said quietly at last. 'The trick is, of course, to recognise the fulfilment of said dream when it actually materialises.'

This time the silence was prolonged and grew tense, and eventually Harriet broke it deliberately, unable to bear it a moment longer.

'So you ran away from your gorgeous widow,' she said lightly. 'You were lucky to find a house like this over here so quickly.'

'Ah, but Torre Branca was already mine. My Monteiro grandmother owned the land outright and left it to me, plus the original farmhouse that went with it. This room and the tower and rooms upstairs were already here, basically. I added and extended over the years— I've always spent part of each year here as my holiday. Reid comes here often as well, and used to keep an eye on the property latterly when my father grew too ill to leave.' Richard poured the last of the wine into their glasses. 'So I'm afraid I'm no longer a farmer. Instead I'm diving headfirst into another venture at the age of thirty-seven. Some might think it foolhardy—do you?'

Harriet thought it over. 'No—no, I don't. This part of

the world is becoming more popular all the time, so th
marina's bound to be a success, surely. By the way, if yo
inherited Torre Branca, what did your brother get?'

'A slice of Monteiro land up in Minho, which he leas
out to a tenant.'

'So now your true colours are revealed at last,' sa
Harriet, and subjected him to a long questioning loo]

Richard met her eyes very directly. 'That's righ
Nothing left to tell—except an entertaining account o
my confrontation with Harvey Jackson. Can yo
imagine my reaction when he told me you threw the jo
in his face the day you got back from your holiday?
could have shaken him by the scruff of his neck, an
must have shown it. I think his secretary thought I wa
going to punch him and looked ready to wade in
protect him.'

'Did she have red hair and freckles?' asked Harrie
with keen interest.

He looked blank, and thought for a moment. 'Yes-
yes, I think she did. Why?'

'Hazel Bishop—she's the one who sent my photograp
to Penry.'

Richard stiffened. 'What did you do about it?'

Harriet shrugged. 'Gave her a lecture, that's all. Let
hope she won't do anything so silly again. Anyway, sh
and Harvey deserve each other. I hope they'll be ve
unhappy together.'

'You should have prosecuted,' he said grimly, the
shot a look at her. 'What has been troubling me, Harrie
is how you got the money together so quickly to send m
that cheque, if you packed in your job.'

She looked down at her hands. 'I made Harvey give m
a month's wages, I sold my car, and I snapped up the firs
job offered to me. I considered moving from my flat, too
but I managed without that in the end.'

'What work are you doing now?'

'I sell weird clothes to the trendy young in Poppy's, th
boutique on the second floor of a department store

Harriet kept her eyes resolutely down, not at all anxious to look Richard in the face.

'You went to great lengths to throw my money in my face,' he observed with bitterness.

'I'm very bad at turning the other cheek. I just had to retaliate, and that was the only form of revenge I could think of at the distance. It was the only way I knew to pay you back for—for——'

'Taking you for the wrong girl?'

She shook her head. 'No. That didn't do the most damage, oddly enough.' She turned to look at him squarely. 'What I really couldn't bear was that after—after that night you could still think I spread myself around. It was a body blow, when you consider that for me it had been the most wonderful experience of my life, while you mistook my naïve enthusiasm for professional expertise. Your manner next day shrivelled my soul.'

Richard winced, and he shook his head as if to clear it of something too unbearable to contemplate. He leaned towards her urgently. 'I know now what a bloody fool I was to be so blind. God knows I wrote to you often enough——'

'Ah, but it took Isabel's embarrassing titbit of information to convince you,' she cut in sharply.

He drew in an unsteady breath. 'Try to understand how it was for me. That night transcended any other experience I'd ever had——'

'And you'd had a fair number!'

'Only the normal count you'd expect for a man of my age.' Richard moved along the sofa and took her hand in his. 'If you remember, you told me you had a lot of men-friends, including the one who wanted to move in with you. I naturally assumed——'

'That I slept with the lot! Charming!' Harriet tried to take her hand away, but he held on to it firmly. 'I have an undeserved reputation among my crowd back home. I've had a number of friendships with men I've liked very

much, but they all ended in the same way, because t'
man got offended when I wouldn't let him into my be
So the popular belief is that I change boy-friends as oft
as I change my clothes, which it totally untrue, but wh
would believe me if I published the facts?'

With great care Richard slid his arm round her wais
and she stiffened for a moment, then relaxed again
him.

'Why *didn't* you let any of them make love to you?' I
asked.

'For the same reason I don't smoke. I've never wante
to. At least, not until . . .' She trailed away, and his ar
tightened fiercely.

'So why did you give yourself to me?' he aske
urgently.

'Is that what I did?' Harriet wriggled round and looke
up at him with mockery in her eyes. 'I don't rememb
much giving—you just took.'

His breathing quickened. 'Why did you let me tal
you, then?'

Her lids dropped instantly. 'I think you know.'

'Tell me,' he said inexorably.

'Because you were the first man I'd felt truly attracte
to in all ways, especially physically, I suppose,' she sa
judiciously, knowing full well it was not what he wante
to hear, but some perverse instinct deep inside her wa
still unwilling to make things smooth for him.

'Who was the man in the photograph sent to Penry
Richard countered, with an irrelevance that startled he

'Why? That photograph was taken three years ago
Harriet stared up at him, marvelling. 'Why should tha
be of any interest to you now?'

His eyes took on a steely look. 'Suffice it to say that
does, nevertheless.'

She sighed impatiently. 'It was Guy, if you must know
my loving brother Guy, who wouldn't be very pleased
he knew the details of my previous holiday in Portugal,
might tell you.'

'Who could blame him?' said Richard sombrely.
'Should I look him up and make a confession about my
spectacular mistake regarding his sister?'

'Lord, no!' said Harriet emphatically. 'The less people
know about that the better. By the way,' she added, 'what
made Penry think I actually was the one when he saw the
photograph?'

'He was still suffering the after-effects of concussion,
and was very hazy about the whole thing. What he really
remembered was seeing the snapshot before, that's all.
The real culprit made off with her own when she ran
from the car. Why are you looking so pensive?' he added.

Harriet gave him a mischievous smile. 'I was just
wondering—sheer feminine pique, you understand—
why Penry preferred the other lady to me!'

Richard shook with laughter and hugged her close.
'The other one was—er—more professional-looking.
You know the sort of thing. Penry said she was heavily
made up, had one of those weird, wild modern hairdo's,
and wore a Miss World-type swimsuit. To him she
appeared more likely to arouse envy in the souls of his
mates than the natural charm of the girl smiling at him
from *your* photograph. You were too much like the other
girls he knew, I'm afraid.'

'Well, thank you, Penry!' Harriet laughed. 'Meeting
you and your relatives has hardly been an ego trip, one
way and another!'

'I could tell you what *I* think of you, if it would help,' he
said, suddenly serious.

Harriet shook her head. 'You don't have to.'

'Why, Miss Neil, I think you're shy!' he teased.

'Which is a happy contrast to what you thought
before!' she retorted.

'Ouch!' Richard jumped up and held out his hand.
'Come on, let's see what Rosa left for me. I told her to
make it light tonight, since I was lunching at the Alba
Mar, so I hope it will do.'

They ate in the kitchen, picnicking on cold pieces of

fried chicken and crisp salad, washed down with more champagne, lingering companionably over the table, and keeping, by common consent, to subjects of a less emotive nature while they ate. Richard enlarged on his plans for the marina with an enthusiasm Harriet found infectious, and she listened, spellbound, to his animated outline of the future. In turn she regaled him with the more hilarious encounters she had experienced with the teenage public at the boutique, and hardly realised how much she had relaxed due to the champagne, until she rose to clear away.

'My knees feel decidedly unco-ordinated,' she said with surprise.

Richard grinned. 'I'll make some coffee, then. I disapprove strongly of drunken guests!'

'How rude.' Harriet cleared the table swiftly, in spite of a slight discrepancy between hand and eye, and washed the dishes against Richard's instructions to leave it all for Rosa. 'Certainly not,' she said. 'Do you have many guests, Richard?'

'Kit and Reid come here a lot, of course, and Kit's family, and one or other of the Monteiros comes down now and again.'

'No friends?'

'I have plenty here, actually, but the others are mainly from my old life in Brazil, and find it a bit far, and a bit expensive, to come very often.' He went ahead with the coffee-tray to the big living-room, which was in darkness by this time. He switched on the lamps on tables flanking the sofa and poured coffee for them both. Harriet curled up in the corner of the sofa again, after kicking off her yellow sandals.

'I hope you don't mind,' she said, waving at her bare feet.

Richard said nothing, and she shifted uneasily.

'Why are looking at me like that?' she asked crossly.

He leaned forward and took her cup away, putting it back on the tray with his own. 'Why did you come back to the Algarve, Harriet?'

'Why did you go to Leamington?' she countered.

'Because I couldn't stand another moment without seeing you. Because I love you so much it hurts, my darling.' Still Richard sat watching her, making no move to touch her.

Harriet's eyes dropped. 'My reason for coming here was much the same,' she said unevenly.

'Much the same?'

'Exactly the same,' she whispered.

'Say it, Harriet—please.'

'I can't in cold blood!' she said in desperation.

'Then there's only one thing to do,' he murmured softly, and in one move he was beside her and she was in his arms and all the skirmishing was over. The first kiss went on and on in a passion of thanksgiving that transcended sexual feelings for a while, until heat rose inevitably in them both with the suddenness of a forest fire.

'Now tell me,' urged Richard against her mouth.

'I love you, I love you . . .' but Harriet said no more as in his triumph his lips cut off the very words he wanted most to hear, and they gave themselves up to the frenzied delight of being in each other's arms at last. Eventually he raised his head to look down into her bemused face.

'Shall I tell you how I felt that night?' he asked breathlessly.

'What night?' Harriet smiled with such teasing effrontery it was some time before he could stop kissing her to continue.

'What I'm trying to say, you witch, is that when I lit the lamp on that never-to-be-forgotten night and turned to see you kneeling there with your hair tumbling over your shoulders I felt as Jason must have felt when he found the Golden Fleece—awe, wonder, disbelief almost, that such perfection should have been granted me.'

Harriet was utterly shaken, and buried her face against his throat. 'Richard,' she said, in a choked voice, 'I won't

always look like this—my hair will go grey and I'll get
scrawny—or fat——'

'Then why are we wasting time!' He tipped back her
face and grinned down into her troubled dark eyes. 'For
God's sake let's get married before decrepitude overtakes
you!'

Harriet's eyes cleared and she laughed with him. 'Are
you asking me to marry you because it's the only route to
my bed?'

Richard rubbed his nose reflectively. 'Would it be very
unchivalrous to remind you that I managed to get there
before without clearance from the church?'

She yanked the cushion from behind her and assaulted
him with it until he cried for mercy, and she halted,
eyeing him. 'What sort of date did you have in mind for
the ceremony?'

'As soon as humanly possible—when else?'

'I've paid for a fortnight's holiday,' she reminded him,
'and I've only had three days or so yet. You played ducks
and drakes with my last holiday, so I'm certainly not
going to cut this one short to dash back to Norwich to get
married.'

'Norwich?'

'Where my parents live, of course!'

Richard lifted her on to his lap and stroked her hair.
'Perhaps we could get round the problem by putting the
cart before the horse.'

'Oh yes?'

He nodded, his eyes very bright as he looked down into
hers. 'We *could*—and it's only a suggestion, mind—have
the honeymoon first and then get married. Seems a pity
to waste ten whole days, since you're so set on having
your holiday.'

'You mean I stay at the Beira Mar and see you in the
evenings?' she asked innocently.

'No. I mean stay here and see me all the time.'

'*Sleep* here?'

'Certainly. In my bed. With me.'

'Do you mean the one in the room with the rude ceiling?'

'You can always close your eyes and think of England!'

Harriet gurgled and nestled closer. 'But how do I know I can trust you to make an honest woman of me afterwards?'

'You don't. You'll just have to take my word for it. But the bed in my room is the one my father had made for my mother when they were first married. It was their marriage bed, if you like, and I was born in it, so was Reid. And you're the first woman I've asked to share it with me.' Richard stood, pulling her up with him, and turned her face up to his. 'Nevertheless, darling, if it would make you happier I'm perfectly willing to wait until we're married before sharing it with you.'

Harriet looked into his eyes for some time, then shook her head. 'Thank you, Richard. I appreciate the offer very much, but I don't think I'll avail myself of it, just the same.'

His face went rigid with shock. 'You mean you won't marry me?'

'What *are* you talking about?' she said impatiently. 'I meant your offer to wait until we're married before——'

'Allowing me the privileges of the marriage bed?' he finished, with such blinding relief on his face Harriet's last doubts about his feelings for her vanished, never to return.

'Well,' she said, with assumed briskness, 'now that's settled perhaps you'd better take me back to the apartment to get my things——'

'Not tonight,' he said firmly, and pulled her towards the door. 'I told you I had a spare toothbrush, and as far as I'm concerned you don't need anything else I can't provide.'

'Very true,' agreed Harriet, and broke free, throwing a glittering look of challenge over her shoulder. 'Last one up the stairs pays a forfeit!'

Richard leapt after her, laughing, but her bare feet

flew to the top of the stairs before his, and she whirled round, breathless, to let him catch her in his arms.

'I concede, you little wretch,' he panted. 'You win. So what forfeit do you want me to pay?'

Harriet stood on tiptoe to link her hands behind his neck. 'I just want you to love me for ever and ever,' she said simply.

He drew in a deep, unsteady breath. 'I thought you were going to ask me something difficult,' he said huskily, and smiled down at her. 'When would you like me to start?'

Harriet shook back her hair from a face alight with mischief. 'Well—now, actually. Unless you've anything better to do!'

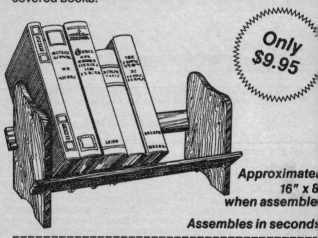